TITAN
A.E.™

A Novel by
STEVE PERRY & DAL PERRY

ACE BOOKS, NEW YORK

TITAN A.E.™

An Ace Book / published by arrangement with
Twentieth Century Fox Animation

PRINTING HISTORY
Ace edition / May 2000

TITAN A.E.™ & © 2000 by Twentieth Century Fox Film Corporation
All Rights Reserved.

The Penguin Putnam Inc. World Wide Web site address is
http://www.penguinputnam.com

Check out the Ace Science Fiction & Fantasy newsletter
and much more on the Internet at Club PPI!

ISBN: 0-441-00736-8

ACE®
Ace Books are published
by The Berkley Publishing Group,
a division of Penguin Putnam Inc.,
375 Hudson Street, New York, New York 10014.
ACE and the ''A'' design are trademarks
belonging to Penguin Putnam Inc.

PRINTED IN THE UNITED STATES OF AMERICA

10 9 8 7 6 5 4 3 2 1

—ACKNOWLEDGMENTS—

As with any novel, no writer is an island. We'd like to thank those who helped with word or deed in the writing of this book.

Our gratitude thus goes to Ginjer Buchanan at Penguin-Ace Books; Melissa Cobb, Virginia King and Angela Nicols, at Fox, Kevin Anderson and Rebecca Moesta, fellow toilers in the word mines; and to the staff at the Jean Nagger Literary Agency, particularly Jean and Joan Lilly this time—and a big hello to Twice-Mama Jennifer, on general principles.

Thanks for the help, folks. We do appreciate it.

"Lead, kindly Light, amid the encircling gloom; Lead me on! The night is dark, and I am far from home . . . "

—JOHN HENRY, CARDINAL NEWMAN

"Home is where the heart is."

—ANONYMOUS

—PROLOGUE—

F ive-year-old Cale Tucker was ready to launch his floater toy. He was so excited that his tummy was doing butterflies. Testing was the most important part of making things, his daddy always said.

"You never know how good your idea is until you try it."

Young Cale had heard that one so many times he'd lost count. At least a hundred.

His daddy ought to know since he built toys too. Lots bigger though.

They'd spent the last night working on the little water craft that Cale now held.

It was called a "gyro-floater" his daddy said, and was made for going on rivers. The stream they had found wasn't really a *river*, but the ship wasn't as big as the pictures they'd looked at to make it, either.

Still, it was beautiful. It was round on top, with a long rod underneath it that went down into the water—everyone was in a hurry today, and his daddy had said they couldn't take long, so they'd made it ready to go.

Everyone seemed to be excited about something that sounded like e-vacation. Cale had been on a few vacations and they'd never seemed that great to him. Lots of sitting in an airplane and then being told to stay away from the water by daddy's friend, the alien called Tek.

This was much more exciting.

Cale leaned down and carefully placed the gyro-floater in the stream. The water wanted to carry it away, but he held it there.

He shifted his grip so he could pull out the control to make it go.

It was hard to pull out, but he did it, being careful not to squeeze too hard.

There.

The little toy shot off down the stream, twirling in the water, *whirr-whirr-whirr . . .*

Cale giggled. Oh, it was *perfect.*

He looked around to see if his daddy saw, and when he looked back, his giggle froze in his throat.

The toy was getting away!

"Hey! Stop that!"

Cale ran off after the gyro-floater. He had to get it!

He ran so fast that he didn't see his daddy until— smack—he'd run right into him. Cale looked up at the sudden obstacle. Daddy!

"Daddy, Daddy! It's getting away! We gotta go get it!"

His daddy reached down and picked him up. But then, instead of moving toward the stream, he started walking *away!*

"Cale, we've got to go now, son."

"But, *Daddy!*"

"We don't have time right now, son, I'm sorry."

Cale had heard that one at least a hundred times too. It meant they wouldn't go back for the toy. And if he yelled too much, they might not make another for a while, either.

"Awww."

His daddy carried him over the top of the hill they'd found the stream on. For the first time that day, Cale began to pay attention to what was going on.

People milled around a whole bunch of silvery rockets, all pointed up at the sky. Men in green clothes helped move everyone along the boarding ramps.

There were hundreds and hundreds of rockets!

Wow.

"Where is everyone going, Daddy?"

"I don't know for sure, son, nobody knows. Somewhere safe, we hope."

"Professor Tucker! Professor Tucker!"

Here came old Tek, yelling, with another man in green clothes. They were in one of the big wide cars with no roof. The car stopped next to Cale and his father, the sudden halt raising a cloud of dust in the hot afternoon air. The car had a funny smell, kind of oily and sharp, and the dust made Cale want to sneeze.

"The Drej have breached the global defense system," Tek said.

His daddy looked at Tek. "Will we be able to get everyone evacuated in time?"

There it was again. E-vacation. Only this time it sounded different. E-vac-u-ated.

"Not if we don't get going, sir." The man in green said. He sounded like he was in a hurry. He sounded mad, too.

Daddy set Cale down in the car and got in.

Wow, now they were going for a ride!

They took off fast, the speed of the ride pushing Cale back into his seat.

Cale looked at the man driving. It didn't look that hard.

"I wanna drive!"

"Not today, kid," said the man, "Maybe if you live until you're older."

"I'm older than four," Cale said, but the man just drove faster.

As they drove, Cale looked around. People seemed to be moving faster now, and running all over the place, everyone in a hurry. He saw someone point up, and Cale took a look, just as it started to get dark.

There was something really, really *big* up there.

The man driving the car did something with a button, and suddenly Cale was pushed back into his seat again. He could hear his daddy talking to Tek.

"Is *Titan* ready?"

"All set to go. Intelligence says the Drej don't know anything about it, or we would have been hit already."

Well the *Drej*, whatever they were, had to be pretty stupid, thought Cale. The *Titan* was daddy's latest ship, and it was so big everyone had to know about it. *He'd* known about it for *months*.

The car jerked to a stop, and Cale was saved from falling forward by his daddy's quick arm.

Recovering, he looked up. Wow.

It was a huge silver rocket. It looked a lot bigger this close up.

He'd never been on a rocket before.

"Are we going to go on that, Daddy?"

"Well, *you* are, son. I have to go on a different ship."

What? "*No*, Daddy!"

"Tek will look after you. You behave, and listen to him."

"But Daddy, I want to go with *you*!"

"I know, son, but it's just not safe where I'm going."

Cale didn't care how safe it was. And he didn't care if he got in trouble for yelling either. His daddy was going to *leave* him!

"I don't care!"

The man in green looked up at the big shadow and then over at his daddy.

"Sir . . . ?"

"Yes, I *know*!" His daddy *yelled* at the man in green.

Then Cale's father held out a ring—a ring that had been on his hand for a long time.

"I want you to take this."

Cale took the huge ring. It looked like it would fit around *all* his fingers.

But no. The ring seemed to grow larger, and then squeezed itself in, *shrinking*.

And it fit on Cale's finger, just as nice as it had Daddy's. Wow. Neat.

"Always keep this, son. It will—I'll—I'll see you later, okay?"

Cale stared at the ring. "Okay."

Suddenly he looked up. His daddy was starting to walk away.

"No! It's *not* okay!"

Cale dived forward and grabbed his daddy's leg. He wrapped his arms around and locked his hands together—tight.

But he was only five, and his daddy was much stronger. After a few seconds he was picked up, crying, and held in a big hug.

His father kissed him on the forehead and then handed him to Tek.

"It'll be all right, son."

And he walked away.

• • •

Cale watched through his tears as his daddy went to one of the elecircles. Once there, he held up his watch-communicator.

Someone must have heard him because the elecircle started to go down.

Cale watched his daddy disappear as Tek carried him up the ramp of the big rocket.

Inside it was darker. Tek took him to the front of the rocket and strapped him down into a very cushy seat. There were all kinds of controls and screens, and for a few seconds Cale was interested enough to try and figure them out. Some showed outside and some showed the ramp, which started to move up as he watched. The air was cold, and it smelled like metal.

There was a great shuddering and a big pressure on his chest, and Cale knew the rocket was moving.

It was hard to breathe for a minute, but then he felt better and looked back out at the screens.

There was one screen that seemed to be showing a big black thing. It was very difficult to see, but Cale thought he could see strange markings on it.

The picture jumped back, and then he saw two more of the big black things.

Giant sparks seemed to move between the ships and then *down*.

The sparks went into the Earth.

Another screen showed a closeup of where they had gotten on the silver rocket. Cale knew it was the same place because he could see the car with no roof and the elecircle where his daddy had gone down.

Just the thought made him sad.

And then on the screen, the ground began to shake, and Cale saw the bright purple sparks from the ship fall and start to zap things. The car went flying away, pieces of it shattered across the now-broken landscape. The sparks blasted big holes in the ground, lots of smoke and fire everywhere.

Tek was saying something. "Come on, Sam! Get out of there! Now! Do it now!"

Yes, Daddy. Get out of there before the purple sparks *get* you!

Suddenly the Earth split apart and a huge rocket, larger than any of the rest of them, shot up into the sky.

Cale knew from all the months he'd seen it, what it was.

Titan!

The ship flew up fast, passing the rockets already climbing into the sky.

The purple sparks got fiercer, and suddenly the entire *world* started to split. Cale looked at another screen, and sure enough, the globe of the Earth was shaking apart.

"Your father made it, son! Yeeeehaww!"

Cale watched the horrible destruction before him. It was awful.

The whole world gone.

Daddy had gone somewhere else without him.

Cale shut his eyes. This was awful. Awful. Awful. . . .

— 1 —

Well, damn.
    The torch was acting up again.

Cale Tucker blinked as a bead of sweat dripped into his eye—despite the fact that it wasn't supposed to happen, it often did. Capillary action, not gravity, did it; the suit circulation was *supposed* to stop that, but of course, it didn't. He was pretty sure that none of the Human vac-suits handed out by their employer, the operators of the lovely Tau-14 salvage station—a nonhuman-owned company with a name he couldn't pronounce—would pass anything other than a cursory safety inspection. If that. And they stank, too. A mixture of the sweat of a thousand gyms, combined with a faint hint of ammonia from the fluid recycler. It was like breathing air strained through dirty old socks.

He used his favorite technique for clearing up the plasma flow in the torch—he slammed it into the side of the hulk he was cutting up.

There, that ought to do it.

He ignited the torch again and cut through the last strut holding the bulkhead in place.

Slice and dice, one more cutoff for the re-sike.

Cale wedged himself between the cutoff and the larger body of the ship and pushed, his effort moving more tons of steel than five cranes could on a planet. Still wasn't easy, the mass and all, but it did move.

"Hey, Zanar! Here comes a big one!"

Zanar Kimble, the recycle catcher for Cale and the other salvage crew on this shift, commed back a quick burst of static on the command channel followed by a quick response.

"Tgod it, Kail."

Now there's a guy who's got a great job.

Catchers, who caught and sent the multiton salvage cutoffs from the ships around Tau-14 to the huge electric furnaces below, were well paid. That they only tended to last a few months on the job was lost on Cale. A typical turnover was the result of a missed salvage item—not too healthy for a catcher.

Wouldn't happen to me.

He watched for a moment as Zanar reached out with huge mechanical arms and shifted the piece toward one of the more distant melts on the surface below. The alien's timing was perfect, and the hunk of salvage made a perfect arc toward melt #4, trailing phosphor paint from the markers Cale had attached earlier.

With the extra pay from catching, he could speed up the schedule for the construction of his ship, *The Escape.* He wasn't going to be stuck on this backwater forever, no way, no how, no matter *what* old Tek said.

Normally, constructing a personal spaceship wasn't the kind of thing that anyone could hope to afford, ever. But Cale had managed to stash away components over his years on the asteroid, and metal was easy to come by in a junkyard like this. Not everything was ready for recycle. At his current rate of construction, though, he wouldn't be launching *The Escape* for at least five years. And even then, it wouldn't be the galaxy's best-looking vessel. What he had so far was, in fact, pretty ugly.

Didn't matter. If it was airtight and it would fly, ugly didn't matter.

But—five years! He'd be an old man of twenty-five by then. Well past his peak, and probably gray-haired to boot.

He'd never attract any girls looking like that.

Not that he'd met many girls in his lifetime. The god-forsaken rock that was Tau-14 didn't have a whole lot of Humans on it, and most of those were salvage crew. The few women he'd met were hard old birds, certainly not the material that his dreams were made of.

Of course, there was that holo program he'd borrowed from Tynan over in section B. Boy would he like to meet someone like her! Tynan had offered to sell it to him for a week's wages, and Cale was still tempted. But that would put him a week behind on *The Escape*, which would make him a week older when he left Tau-14.

Decisions, decisions, all the time.

He turned from watching Zanar to his next cutoff and fired up the torch. He wouldn't make any more money wishing he had another job.

Catcher was a position that always went to aliens anyway.

Sometimes he hated being Human.

Nnneeehh!

The lunch buzzer!

Cale winced from the deafening blast in his helmet. He held the wince because he knew what was coming.

"That's LUNCH! ONE hour for LUNCH!"

The grizzled voice of Chowquin, the foreman, was almost as bad as the buzzer.

Cale deactivated the power cell of his torch and left it hanging in space. He activated his magnetic boots and got to the scooter.

The early salvage crews had used compressed air to shoot down to the surface, but this resulted in too much time lost to rate-of-descent miscalculations in the form of injured salvage crews, particularly on first workday, so management had constructed a huge tower that jutted up to the salvage yards above the asteroid, with an elevator in the middle. And they'd given the crews small, one-person reaction scooters to get to their stations and back.

Unfortunately, this meant waiting your turn in the salvage hierarchy. Cale, like all the other Humans, was at the bottom. Lowest of the low, Humans, no planet to call their own, always in the back of the transport.

As the last nonhumans were getting into the elevator, Cale brought his scooter to a neat stop.

Perfect.

Just as he was about to catch himself on the rim of the interior door, Cale jolted to a stop. *Huh?*

Chowquin. One of his massive hands held Cale by the back of his helmet.

"Hey!"

"Uh, hey, yourself, Chowquin. How ya hittin' 'em?"

"You wait," said the huge alien.

"Hey, it's me, Cale, all right? I'm not with those *losers*." He waved at those still standing in line.

"Humans wait," came the grating voice.

Cale sometimes wished the Drej had finished the job they'd started on Earth so many years ago.

Why the Drej had decided to destroy the home of mankind had never been determined. Galactic justice being what it was, no one had been a strong enough ally of Humanity to call them on it and find out. If anybody really cared.

Mankind had been real surprised to discover that the rule of the mighty held true in the whole galaxy. Law of the jungle. Only the strong survive.

For whatever reason, the Drej had decided that with no home as a base, Humanity—or what was left of it—wasn't worth bothering about.

And as a rootless species, with no land of their own, and no resources to call upon, the Drej seemed to be right about mankind. Humans had become dependent on the generosity of strangers. This too had mirrored earlier findings on Earth—as the immigrants everywhere they went, they got the worst jobs at the worst pay.

Like this crappy job.

Cale felt himself suddenly accelerate, scooter and all, toward the Humans waiting for the next elevator. Chowquin had *thrown* him.

The waiting Humans scattered, but not all of them made it out of Cale's way before he hit.

"Hey, watch it!"

"Welcome back to the losers," came a voice on his comm.

"Don't count on it, pal," said Cale, his embarrassment turning to anger. "You wait in line if you want. *I'm* taking the express."

Cale pointed his scooter "downspace" toward the elevator tower.

"You idiot kid!" came another voice on the comm. "You go through the docks and you'll get yourself killed!"

"You *are* a loser," Cale commed back. "The odds of a ship docking are more'n a thousand to one!" Stupid losers, no guts, no—uh-oh. He looked around.

Bad thing about the helmets was how they messed

with your peripheral vision. How could he have missed
it?

Cale watched as the huge ship moved to intersect his
flight and smash him.

So much for the odds. "Damn! Where did you come
from?"

This was, in a word, bad.

Well, he'd never had a ship come in when he'd taken
the elevator shortcut before. This would make for some
interesting discussion with Tek over lunch. Assuming he
survived to eat lunch.

He'd made the jump between elevator shafts twice
before, no sweat. He'd touched down, had been the first
Human to lunch, and up yours, pals.

The problem was that both he and the ship wanted
the same airlock, so there was a very likely chance that
they would cross paths. Or intersect.

Although weightless, the mass of the ship would still
crush him if he got between it and the airlock, and if he
got hit, he risked being knocked out into space. Then it
would be bye-bye Cale, 'cause nobody on this friggin'
rock would come after him, 'cept maybe Tek, and *he*
sure wasn't up to it, being blind and all.

Maybe this wasn't such a good idea.

Fine. Now *you* think of that.

Here came the ship. It plainly wasn't just a deepspace
craft. Sleek lines and extended airfoils meant it could
maneuver in-atmosphere as well. It was gorgeous. Look
at that! Six thrust engines surrounding a warp core.
Wow!

With warp, the ship could go *any*where.

Cale realized the ship was closer now. A lot closer.

It sure looked like they were going to intersect.

His current motion relative to the ship seemed to be
slower. This meant any impact would be bad.

It *was* bad. The scooter slammed into the nose of the incoming ship, and he flipped off, bouncing along the hull toward the front viewport.

Oof!

It was like getting punched in the gut, hard. But—

He grinned anyway. He wasn't gonna eat vac today!

He activated his boots and walked toward the viewport. In-atmosphere ships always had a port.

Now who was flying a beauty like this? Cale reached the port and looked in.

Oh, my.

It was another kind of beauty.

A girl!

And a girl not like any other he'd ever seen. She was gorgeous, an elvin face framed by long strands of dark hair. Almond shaped eyes focused on the control panel.

Wow. She was *better*-looking than the holo program he'd borrowed from Tynan. Much better.

Cale felt a mild bump and realized that they'd docked. *Nice landing.*

He leaned forward to get a closer look at the angel flying the ship and—*clunk*—rapped his helmet against the kleersteel of the cockpit.

She must have heard the vibration because she looked up. A very long moment hung there as she narrowed her eyes and frowned. Thinking fast, he pulled a rag from his suitbelt and pretended to wipe the viewport. That ought to make her smile.

The beautiful pilot remained expressionless as she reached over and pressed a button, then disappeared as micrometeorite-armor shutters slammed down, covering the portal.

Hey—!

So much for the clean portal gambit. Nice to meet you, too.

If not better, it was certainly starting to be a more interesting lunch than it had started out to be.

Cale headed for the airlock. He grinned. So he'd almost gotten squashed—he was gonna be the first Human at lunch. Ha!

— 2 —

Akima checked the warp core readout again as the *Valkyrie* approached Tau-14. Just as they had last time, the readings indicated that the core was off-line.

Always check twice.

She'd heard the words first from a woman named Porter, her first flight instructor back on Houston colony. Over the years she'd spent working her way up as a pilot, Porter's training had served her well. Piloting a starship was not a task for the detail-challenged. A mistake could be fatal. Fatal was bad.

A ship like the *Valkyrie* was more complex than most. No less than three drive systems were needed: first to get the powerful craft off a planet, then through deep space, and *then* through warp space.

Fortunately, Akima was well trained and experienced in all three types of flight.

She'd been four when her family had left Earth, and had a few memory holos of that first trip into space. One was very clear, a man pointing at a control panel, the shiny plastic of the panel glinting in the dim shiplights, and the faint smell of hot electronics.

There was something about it that had stuck with her. Something *good* about controls.

Controls could *take* her places.

She'd begun training as soon as she was old enough, but that wasn't possible. It hadn't been easy just surviving.

Her family had been split up in the mass exodus from Earth, those who made it at all, and her grandmother alone had supported her when they reached the drifter colonies.

The Earther ships had run as far as they could from the devastating Drej. Other aliens, who had befriended Humanity, who had been so helpful when there were enough resources to be had, grudgingly granted leases to minor moons or asteroids in a variety of systems—at a price, of course.

The ships that had run were joined into huge orbiting colonies over these rocks. Huge orbiting colonies with little or sometimes no future.

Naturally, the aliens had given the Humans the very worst of their real estate; what minerals and resources the drifters managed to scrounge went straight into maintaining the colonies. Making a profit had to come from somewhere else. Like most places with few resources, a variety of options had been tested.

Some of the colonies tried gambling. Others, like Houston, worked to develop a labor pool that could be hired. Nobody was much impressed with Humans, but if they could do the job, and do it cheaper, they'd get hired.

Vast electronics sweatshops had sprung up early on in the colony's history. Akima's grandmother had worked in one for years, straining her sight and hands to assemble components for alien computers.

It hadn't been easy, no. And her grandmother had not

let her quit what education was available for her to work, either.

"I will not become a burden to you, my granddaughter," she had explained. "You must not be fettered with such things."

At first, Akima had believed that her grandmother wanted to live vicariously through her—that by being freed from a financial burden, she would somehow live out her grandmother's desire to be free of responsibility.

She had been wrong.

"My child, you must believe me the most doting of old women if you truly think I have worked all my life simply to fulfill your dreams of flight."

Akima had waited.

"Your ambition will carry the added weight of my own. You will be away from this place. Travel as far as you can, and always seek out a way to end *this*."

The old woman, who had never shed a tear, nor shown any anger during the years of struggle that they had endured on the colony, had slammed her hand down on the metal dining table in their common room so hard that it had knocked over the ceramic salt and pepper shakers of Mt. Fuji and Gojira.

"If you ever find a way to give us a home again, a world that is ours, you must take it. Travel far and wide, my child, and never stop looking."

With that, her grandmother then smiled sweetly and offered her a cup of green tea.

Akima winced at the memory.

Gee, thanks Granny, now I get to spend the rest of my life looking for another home for Humanity. Big improvement.

Well. Enough of this memory jam. Back to work.

She called up the read of Tau-14's docking setup. It

was time to disengage the autopilot and prepare for touchdown. She waved the visual scans to life. *Here we are....*

Part of the scan showed an exterior of the salvage station buried into the rock of Tau-14.

It was one of the most decrepit place she'd ever seen. *Well, scratch* this *place as a future home.*

They didn't even have a live dock-controller. Of course, since this rock probably didn't get many ships other than ones that were being torn apart, that made a certain amount of sense. Still, it was a trash heap, a beyond-salvage dump. Who would live here if they didn't have to?

What could her new boss possibly *want* here?

Korso had kept quiet about their goal, and Akima hadn't wanted to pry. She'd been so excited to be handling a ship of the *Valkyrie*'s caliber that she hadn't wanted to jam the tubes in the slightest. Who cared what he wanted, when you got right down to it? As long as she got to fly this baby, she'd take him anywhere he wanted to go.

Korso's previous pilot, a saureen named Djawana, had apparently been somewhat unreliable, and when Korso stopped at Houston, he'd been in the pilot's lounge within minutes looking for a replacement.

Akima had been a week out from her last job, flying a crappy freighter between Houston and Spartan, just a system away. The freighter, the *Peharu Dalam*, had been a cheesy piece of junk, space-going flotsam that leaked air and radiation like a sieve, but even so, it had been hands-on experience with the warp drive, and any ride was better than none. Unfortunately, the second officer had started indicating his interest in docking his own vessel with her. This wouldn't have been so bad if he hadn't tried to do it while she was on watch. A few near misses with some micrometeorites and Akima had been forced to use some of the jujitsu holds her grandmother had passed on to her with the family art.

The captain had been unhappy to find his second mate reduced to sitting in a sling in sick bay, pumped full of orthobond to set his broken bones, and had fired her. Fortunately, that had been back at Houston, and she'd had a place to stay while she looked for more work. So she'd stopped by the pilot's lounge on her way to Stith's, just to check the board behind the bar to see if any new positions had come up.

There weren't any new jobs posted, but then Korso had stormed into the lounge, a man in a big hurry.

"I need a pilot qualified for air, intra-, and extra-system, ready to go in ten minutes," he'd said, his voice booming out to the mostly empty lounge. He was an interesting looking man, dark, muscular, with a thin beard and a knowing smirk.

Akima had gotten to her feet, smiled, and answered his challenge, her everpresent ship's bag beside her. She recognized him immediately—even if he didn't seem to remember her. He was Korso, friend of Sam Tucker, the man who delivered Professor Tucker's final logs to Mohammed Bourain at New Marrakech just before the Drej attack.

"Let's jet," she'd said.

"You're qualified? A Human?"

"I am. You don't happen to need a gunner, do you?"

"Actually, I could use one."

"I have just the girl for you. Best Weapons Specialist in the colony."

"That's probably not saying much."

"She's a Mantrin."

"Oh, well, in that case, bring her along."

Stith would love this.

Korso had seemed surprised to see a Human who met all of the piloting requirements, but within ten minutes after checking her logged hours in the pilot's registry and settling on a salary, they'd left for the *Valkyrie*.

Stith bitched about the hurry-up, but the chance to run a ship's guns got her there in six minutes flat. Mantrins *lived* to shoot.

They had launched immediately. It wasn't until they'd made deep space and popped into warp that she'd had the chance to meet the rest of the crew.

With the exception of Korso, they were all aliens.

At least she wouldn't have to worry about the kind of problem she'd had on the freighter. Unless the aliens were perverts.

Korso didn't seem like he'd be a problem in that area either. He was driven by something, pushed to meet some kind of internal deadline. The man was in a hurry wherever he went. He'd never be able to find the *time* to bother her.

Preed, Korso's first mate, was a quiet, dangerous looking Akrennian. Akima supposed part of that dangerous look had to do with the fact that he was missing an ear and part of his skull. According to Preed, he'd lost those parts fighting a slaver some years before. The loss made his elongated, baboonlike head look uglier than it already was. Which was remarkably ugly.

Stith, the Mantrin master gunner had always reminded Akima of a cross between two terrain animals she'd seen in a picture book in her childhood, a kangaroo, and a bird—she had a huge beak for a mouth and heavy, muscular legs and tail. The Mantrin race were known for their ability to make war, so Korso was lucky to have her on board. Stith could shoot the eye out of a flea at fifty paces, and you pick which eye . . .

This would be a dangerous ship, even though it hadn't been designed with that purpose in mind.

Gune, the remaining member of the crew, had filled her in on the ship's history. It had been built on Earth, as a space yacht for some ultra-rich corporate leader. Over the years it had belonged to several less-legitimate business dealers, and had been refitted with pulse cannon and missile launchers.

Akima wished that Gune would fill her in on his history. She'd never seen anything that looked like him before. Huge eyes glistened behind thick optitronic flat-screens that kept the odd little alien from having to do more than glance at the viewscreens in his work area near engineering. Korso had explained that Gune was going to help them navigate, but Akima hadn't seen much of him so far.

The trip to Tau-14 had been a straight shot, easy to calculate, and Gune had only nodded when Akima had discussed the jump.

"It is well," he'd said, before going back to some kind of experiment that cluttered several of the control panels. Akima had asked what he was working on, and the alien's eyes had brightened for a minute before beginning a long discourse on nanomachine delivery and re-generative power supplies.

After the first few seconds Akima had been lost, but kept smiling.

The alien genius had seemed satisfied with her attention and had turned back to his work at some invisible prompt from his flatscreen lenses.

Akima disengaged the autopilot and noted their current rate of deceleration, attitude toward the docking clamps, and distance to travel.

Only about a thousand meters. Easy as breathing.

Many pilots preferred to let the the autopilot bring them in, but since this was Akima's first touchdown in the *Valkyrie*, she wanted to see how the ship handled.

She triggered the docking jets, releasing minute amounts of compressed air to correct a minor imbalance in their attitude.

It wasn't much, the autopilot would have got them in at this angle, but she wanted *her* landing to be *perfect*.

Might as well show my new boss he's getting what he pays for.

There was a pinging sound and Korso's face appeared in the heads up display just to the right of her line of sight. The ship's designers had done well in their positioning of commo. Wouldn't do to have him suddenly appear in front of her at a crucial moment of flight.

Speak of the devil.

If fact, now that she thought about it, Korso did kind of resemble a brown-haired version of the devil. Just add horns and a tail. . . .

"Pilot, let me know as soon as we're locked down," Korso said. "I want to get our package as soon as possible and get off this rock."

Akima couldn't have agreed more. The prospect of another flight so soon excited her as well.

Looks like I'll be checking out some more real estate.

They were close now. Akima could see the flashing green lights of the docking clamps. The sensors in the clamps would be flashing amber or even red if her approach were a danger to the docking elevator. Green, green, and green, right on target.

She double-checked everything, of course. There were no discrepancies.

Almost there now.

Akima watched the distance and deceleration readout and slowly pulled back on the joystick.

Compressed air slowed their advance to less than a few millimeters a second and the docking clamps kissed with only the tiniest of bumps.

Excellent, if she did say so herself.

Akima signaled the computer at the station to go ahead and extend the accordion that would connect the two airlocks, and began checking her readouts.

—Clump—

What was that?

Akima looked around at her controls and then at the kleersteel portal.

There was a spacesuited figure outside peering in at her.

What the hell?

The figure leaned closer and she could make out that it was a Human—a male about her age. He smiled at her and waggled his eyebrows. Then he pulled out a red rag and made as if to wipe the kleersteel portal.

She wanted to smile, but she kept her face impassive. It wouldn't do to let this apparition see he'd gotten a point from her.

Akima leaned to her left and punched the button that activated the micrometeorite shields.

There was a faint vibration, and she saw the figure vanish as the shields snapped down.

Check that *action, window-wiper.*

Now she smiled as she commed Korso.

"We're in and attached, Captain. Lockdown."

"Nice work, Akima. Keep her hot, and keep your eyes open. I'll be in touch."

Akima stretched as she walked to the tiny storage locker behind the pilot's chair to get a cold drink.

She was pleased. Good flight, good touchdown, and a happy captain.

Excellent.

If she could keep this up, she'd be flying this bird forever. Not a bad thought, not at all.

— 3 —

Susquehana, Keeper of the Orb, Shaper of the Will, and Queen of the Drej, considered her current problems with the focus and intensity that had allowed her to rise to where she had risen. Part of that focus required that she keep in touch with things past, for to forget the past was demonstrated folly. All things must be puzzled together for the larger picture to be seen. Anything less than the large picture was the way to ruination.

She ruminated. She considered the old saying: *Isssah lalli jee quan mati.*

For any may become Queen.

Her own plans came to such fruition a mere two Makings ago. Before then, she had been merely *droheh*, a heightened drone, subfocus of the then-Keeper-and-Shaper's energies, and an efficient, if not particularly distinguished, carrier of the Will. Although it was true that any might be Queen, most of the time it was a heightened drone like herself who had the capacity to imagine and execute their way to the post. It was not a road taken lightly, and hidden and deadly pitfalls lay thereon. A wrong step brought a quick end. Rewards were great, but risks were many.

Her brain calculated at incredible speeds, as did those of all her people. They were creatures of light, after all, light integrated into fleshy envelopes by the mother Drej, focused to do the race's will.

Which was essentially *her* will now, so far as it went.

There were limitations, to be sure. The power of the Orb, assumed when the former mother died, worked only to further the ends of the race. The Orb, an artifact created by the earliest Drej, was a technological check on her power, a binding commitment to serve, rather than benefit personally.

Which was fine, since that was what Susquehana desired to do anyway. But she sometimes considered what would happen when the Drej *did* rule this galaxy. Would there be time for other things? Would the bounds of the Orb alter?

Madness, of course. What is there, except duty?

Her race was the most perfect in this universe, much less this galaxy. They suffered no disease, did not need to ingest fuel, lived for thousands of years, and were not afflicted with that *disgusting* need to procreate. They existed to serve, to expand, to go forth, and occupy all.

They were duty.

That they might or might not be native to this galaxy, or perhaps even to this universe, was not an issue. Purity was purity, and the Drej intended to spread their light across all they could find, as always they had.

As the Mother, that was her goal and her responsibility, and as ever, there were threats to that responsibility.

Primary was the ongoing problem concerning the race incubator, her ship, *Alahenena*. This was an issue that had plagued Queens before her. The vessel was huge, a warp-capable ship larger than most moons. It was powerful; entire worlds had been extinguished by its primary weapons. The ship's appetite for energy was colossal, and, unfortunately, the dangers of their current source of energy were becoming almost as large.

The *Alahenena* was powered by a captured whitedwarf star. The star emitted energy at strange frequencies, enough to feed the needs of the Drej race: the Makings, the operation of the vessel, and the destruction of their enemies.

Not even she really knew where the energy emitted by the star came from; some of the technical *drohehs* speculated that it came from another universe. If so, it wasn't one that the Drej had yet visited. Perhaps it simplified a missing-matter equation somewhere.

It was not a concern really, the Drej didn't need to know where it came from, so long as the energy flowed.

The problem was the container the white dwarf sat in. It was failing.

The early Drej to this sphere had come and prepared the nucleus of the *Alahenena*. They had captured the white dwarf, set up the Orb, and created other Artifacts for Makings. One gave the Queen the ability to call forth the light of the Drej from the limitless universe: energy and light into living matter—more Drej. The other gave the Queen the ability to manipulate inert matter.

The basins holding the white dwarf were fashioned from energies whose properties could not be found naturally in the universe. They had been painstakingly worked out by the Drej over millennia while in their home galaxy—the plans for these properties, alas, had not been included in the matrix for the new ship from which Susquehana reigned.

The problem was that the Artifact had been damaged during the destruction of an early Drej colony. A suicidal pack of biologicals had blown up most of the planet to do so. The result had been less than they would have hoped, for the Artifact still functioned. But the Artifact had been damaged. The energy basins surrounding the white dwarf! had become—for want of a better term— misaligned.

Unfortunately, Drej philosophy being what it was, no one had considered that the irreplaceable Artifact could ever be damaged. The Drej colonization project had been provided with a powerful Artifact, but no theory on repair or creation of new ones, since there would never be a need. And there was no way to contact home for repairs. The thought had apparently been that, without the theory, an enemy could never duplicate their greatest weapons.

Susquehana wondered how many Queens had cursed that particular decision. Certainly she had.

She called up a drone's-eye view of the current state of the problem.

The Orb let her see from any drone or *droheh* in the galaxy, which was useful for many things.

A huge number of drones swarmed around special shielding that had been manufactured using the damaged inert-matter Artifact. Their partially luminous bodies glowed with internal light as they moved the pieces of black shielding into place.

The failing energy basin had been leaking dangerous radiation for a long time, and a path had been cleared to let it leak into space. The shielding was not so efficient as the original patterns, however, and it had to be replaced. Constantly. A great many materials had been tried to better shield efficiency, but none had fared as well as even what the damaged artifact could produce.

Susquehana watched them work for a moment with a

small portion of her light as she considered the related matter of Heshach, Scout drone Zil-three.

Scout drone Zil-three, called informally "Heshach," prowled through the underground facility on the planet called Earth.

He was an advanced-model drone, capable of infiltrating most biospheres. His light-filled body was covered with a dark coating of *sglum*, a natural collector of light, and one that rendered him impervious to most sensor arrays.

He would not fail in his mission.

He crept around small wooden boxes and metal cages filled with all kinds of bioforms. He did not know why the Queen wished to see this ugly bioplace, but that was not his concern, nor an impediment to his duty.

He watched.

A Human leaned over the table and made an adjustment to a console there. The Human said, "Sam Tucker, test adjustment three-oh-five, seven-seven calibration."

Then the-Human-Sam-Tucker focused a small concave dish on a box at the other end of the table. Heshach could sense that the box contained a wide variety of materials.

A series of latch switches were thrown next, and the lights in the room dimmed as a thin blue haze began to appear around the element box.

Almost immediately an orange mist began to appear on the opposite end of the table. Within the mist was an indistinct shape.

The-Human-Sam-Tucker shut off the latch switches and stepped back around the shield he'd gone behind. There on the opposite side of the table sat a box which looked *exactly* like the one he'd pointed the accumulator at.

"Eureka!" cried Sam. "I've got it!"

He leapt up and danced around the room.

Unfortunately, this activity knocked over sets of boxes, thus revealing the hidden Hesasch.

The Human stared at the alien in shock.

"Korso—!" he yelled.

There was a blur of motion at the edge of the drone's perception—

And then Hesasch saw no more as a series of bolts from a particle accelerator removed his—and therefore his Queen's—eyes from the scene.

Susquehana stopped playback of the recorded memory. The Queen at the time had recognized the obvious danger.

Biobods had discovered Artifact technology.

Her conclusion had been fast and decisive.

Eradicate them.

So the Earth had been destroyed just as soon as the *Alahenena* could reach it.

When Sam Tucker's ship, the *Titan*, slipped through the net of Drej stingers, the Queen had lost focus, convinced that the ship would be the genesis of Drej destruction.

Another heightened drone, Molalah, had picked that moment to challenge the Queen. The drone had succeeded in destroying the Queen and taking her place.

Molalah had been reluctant to commit any more resources to the final destruction of the Humans. Her conclusion, after reviewing the pertinent data, was that the previous Queen had been mistaken. There had been no recreation of the box, but a clever hoax set up for the Drej, perhaps to keep them wary of the upstart biobods. A costly ruse for the Humans in that their planet had been destroyed as a result, and they had been scattered across the galaxy.

Careful watch was kept over the next several years, but the *Titan* seemed to have vanished completely, and no sign of Sam Tucker or the so-called technology was seen again.

The connection that neither of her predecessors had made however, was that *if* the Humans had Artifact technology, *if* it was no hoax, the Drej could use it to repair their Artifact.

And to make many more *Artifacts.*

They could easily repair the damage to the white dwarf's basin, and with more than one device to control matter, the Drej would be unstoppable. They would devour the light of this galaxy within only a few dozen Makings.

So Susquehana had started looking for clues as to the whereabouts of *Titan*, the ship that Sam Tucker was supposed to have been on on the last day of Earth.

Wherever you are, Human, I will find you, and if you have what we need, I will take it.

She had already sent drones looking for *Titan*, as well as anyone related to Sam Tucker in any way.

They would find *something.*

Susquehana shuttled her perception to a series of inanimate viewpoints near the communications grid and considered the ability of her race to match others in baseline stupidity.

To register in any comparison, there must be a common zero.

True.

But it annoyed her to consider just how amateurish the assassins who waited for her today really were.

I deserve better.

There were risks to being Queen. It was the most honored task a Drej could undertake, of course, but also the most dangerous.

At any time an assassin could kill you. This would be proof of the assassin's qualification to assume the job, and after removing the Orb from the corpse and ingesting it, said assassin would then become the most powerful Drej.

But they would have to be very good to get that far. The Orb, after all, allowed the possessor to see what any would-be assassin could see. A careful plotter would have to be so unsuspected as to never be checked upon.

And so, even though any *may* be Queen, only the most intelligent and cunning *would* achieve that.

Certainly not these *fools.*

Susquehana studied the communications area. A series of consoles were bridged with biobod technology so that the Drej could keep track of their inferiors. Two *droheh* were stationed at the receiving grid. One, Lakish, was a senior analysis drone, who had called Susquehana to set up the briefing. She suspected that the plot was his. His obvious ploy for her to come to the commo room immediately was transparent in the extreme. One did not rush a Queen.

The other *droheh*, Quahan, was a slightly modified listening drone who had recently been in the field looking for clues to the *Titan*. A nothing.

Several *deeheh* with focus burners were stationed near the door.

A sorry scheme. When I arrive to speak to the droheh, *they will attempt to extinguish me. Could they really be that stupid?*

Another *droheh* stood near an input locus to the back of the large room. It was monitoring the current ship traffic in this quadrant. Nothing unusual there—then

Susquehana noticed a slight irregularity about the *droheh* in the input locus. It was *leaning* strangely.

She used the Orb to see from its eyes.

There was nothing at first, just the unfocused stare that she expected. After a few pulses she prepared to move her focus. And then—

The eyes shifted slightly down and to the right.

Susquehana saw what the *droheh* did: a modified tripod burner between the *droheh* and the console. Out of sight from any inanimate point of focus for the room, but he had to shift slightly to keep it hidden.

Aha!

Not a great plot, but better than she'd thought. The *deeheh* were a decoy. The tripod burner was the real threat.

Or was it? If Lakish had been clever enough to plant the *deeheh* as decoys with a backup, perhaps there was another danger.

Susquehana studied the room further. Using the Orb she called up a schematic of the room's energy points and traced the current functions. No obvious tampering.

Well.

It seemed the tripod was the best they could do. Not nearly good enough.

She cleared a path between her chamber and the comm room and called upon another function of the Orb. It could be caused to create visual transparency, routing light from one side of her to the other, making her effectively invisible. Thus cloaked, she went forth.

When she reached the comm room, Susquehana moved to put herself on the opposite side of the *droheh* from the tripod burner. There she uncloaked, first her huge luminous eyes, light bursting forth as from a tiny pair of white suns.

She triggered the inanimate viewpoints as she did so;

best to broadcast this to other would-be Mothers.

There was a gasp from one of the *droheh:* Quahan.

Well, surprise, surprise. Lakish was also startled, but not as much as Quahan. *Ah, it seems I was mistaken. Quahan is the would-be assassin.*

There was no harm in being wrong. She would attempt to figure out how Quahan had manipulated Lakish into sending her the message. It was a clever ploy, no doubt picked up from his time with the biobods.

It didn't matter now. Now it was time for action.

"*Ahan jehas lalli jee quan mati?*" she said to the group.

So you wish to be Queen?

Though rare, a formal challenge could be initiated by members of an ascension plot. If the challenge were issued by the challenger, it conferred an extra point of distinction should they succeed. To take on the Queen with the limited resources of a regular drone and to say so publicly was bold indeed. Conversely, to discover a plot and reveal it this close to implementation showed a degree of style as well.

Quahan didn't even try to deny it.

"Eha!" he cried. He lunged for the console, no doubt scrabbling for a hidden weapon—

The Orb gave the Queen an ability to use natural light at an increased intensity that did not require a focus burner to magnify into a deadly ray.

Three beams of coherent light joined her with the *droheh* in the input focus, as well as the two *deeheh* who were fast enough to lift their burners, but slightly before she extinguished their lights with her own.

Quahan reached the console and may have had enough time to actually touch the weapon underneath before the Queen removed his head in a fan of focused light. What he had been flared up and painted the walls in a bright flash, then was gone.

Lakish merely bowed his head and waited.

Loyal, Lakish, but stupid.

She could always make more like him.

Still, she would accord him some honor. She moved forward and became fully visible now. As the Queen, the Orb had given her a greater stature than any normal drone, even the deadliest *deeheh*. She extended her right arm and from her fingers protruded the glassy blades that were a Queen's traditional, ceremonial method of combat.

The blades were exceedingly sharp. She opened Lakish with a single swipe, allowing his light to flow free.

Susquehana lifted her head up to face the inanimate viewpoints she had activated to record her challenge for all Drej to see.

"Ahni sali jahal Drej!" she said.

The Drej continue.

She allowed herself an expression of triumph.

Let them see, she thought, *let them understand that they are led by a leader who will not lose.*

It was too bad that she could not broadcast this to all of the biobod inferiors who opposed her. Not that it mattered.

They would find out soon enough anyway.

—4—

C ale could *smell* it long before he saw it.

The commissary gave the salvage workers all they could eat—which wasn't much most of the time, given the way their alien chef prepared what was jokingly referred to as food. The place was down a dozen levels into Tau-14. On balance, Cale figured it was pretty smart to bury it so deep. Not because of the safety factor, being protected from micrometeor strikes while eating or anything, but because any new salvage workers coming into the station would turn around and haul butt if they saw what lay in store for them, foodwise. . . .

This way, they had to get so many levels away from whatever shuttle had dropped them off, they usually wouldn't make it back in time to catch the flight out.

I hope the smell doesn't scare her *away.*

Even though the beautiful pilot had been, ah, well, a bit *aloof* with her quick slamming of the meteor shutters, Cale hoped he'd see her again. Once she got to know him, surely she'd see the error of her ways. He wasn't so bad.

As he neared the commissary, the sudden odor became acidic, with a slight hint of chlorine, a dash of a stopped-up centrifuge toilet, and just a *touch* of burnt insulation. Of course, it all smelled pretty much alike, the handful of standard slops that Cook routinely wrought, but Cale thought he recognized this particular stink.

It could *be synthflesh in jelly sauce....*

Naw—last time Chowquin had that one, Cook had bruises the next day.

Gotta be ET meatballs.

ET meatballs was a name the Humans had given to the meat with red sauce Cook had concocted as a dual Human/nonhuman delight. Since many of the nonhumans on Tau-14 had a desire for real meat as opposed to the vat-grown synthflesh preferred by the Humans, the little scarab-faced alien, known none-too-affectionately as Cook had gotten, so he thought, *inventive*. He'd found some protein-laden grubs eating one of his shipments of organics and instead of squashing them, he had *bred* them. The little critters weren't too bad when well-cooked, kinda crunchy and salty, but Cook liked to fix his meals rare. This tended to make ET Meatballs, well, call it an ... *interesting* dish at times. As far as Cale could tell, Cook could char stuff impaled on a stick over an open fire for all it mattered as to how good it would taste.

Cale walked into the dining area. Yep, there it was, ET meatballs. He grabbed an oversized tray and lifted it over his head as he moved into the chow line.

The serving area had been designed for a race of aliens much taller than Humans. Taller than some of the aliens here, too, which suited Cale fine.

Let them *feel what it's like to be last on the elevator.*

Cale felt a splash as some of the red sauce rained down on him. Cook was not the most careful of servers. The little alien chattered on as he served the meatballs, oblivious to any responses he got:

"How ya doin' today? Working hard? Well, bon petit! You deserve the best, and the best is what I got! Hey, keep the line movin'! Next! How ya doin'?"

Cale wondered if Cook really believed he had the best food around.

Well, think about it, spud, he does, since it's the only *food around.*

Cale lowered his tray and eyed the gooey melange. Using his finger, he thumped the tray.

One of the "meatballs" hopped off the tray and made a run for it.

Great.

"Hey, Cook! You got any ketchup?" Cale said

"Ketchup? Ketchup! You don't need ketchup! Please! Next!"

"Well how about some *ketch-it*!" Cale called back. He waved at the fleeing meatball.

Nobody laughed. The joke was as old as the asteroid.

Cale shrugged and made his way toward the table where he usually sat with Tek, the old alien with whom he'd been left for so many years.

Sure enough, there was Tek, reading his ancient, out-dated braillecomp, the little device's touchscreen providing a tactile series of images and text for those who could interpret it. A salvage accident some years ago had left Tek blind.

Cale sat down and thumped his tray hard against the table. Another of his meatballs mistook the jolt as a starting gun and fled for the edge of the table.

"I don't think I'm asking a lot," he said. "I just want

my food all the way *dead* before they serve it to me. Is that too much for a fella to ask?"

"Ahh, Cale arrives and peaceful dining flees in terror," Tek said. "Hmm. Do you hear a crackling sound?"

Oblivious, Cale carried on. "And take Chowquin. You should have seen him!"

"Not much chance of *that*," murmured Tek.

"What was up with *him* today? He treated me like . . . like—"

"A Human," said Tek.

Yeah. There it was. Human. Thanks for the support, Tek.

Cale glared. Of course his alien guardian couldn't see him, but it felt good anyway.

"Don't start that old solidarity rap again, Tek," said Cale. "Yeah, if Humans were all together, it'd be great, but it ain't happening, and I sure won't see it in *my* lifetime."

"If you would only study your history, Cale, or at least *remember* what I've taught you, you might realize you're not alone. Humans have faced incredible odds in their history and prevailed. If you remember this, you might be better prepared for the future."

Cale took advantage of his mentor's blindness and started making faces at him while the old alien continued his diatribe.

Blah blah blah know-it-all-Tek. If you're so smart, what are you doing on this crummy station with me?

Finally he couldn't stand the lecture anymore.

"Well *I'll* tell you something about your famous 'future,' Tek. Every day we wake up in *this* gritty, boring, present, *stuck* here. I don't think this great 'future' exists."

Cale paused.

What was that noise? "Do you hear a crackling sound?"

Tek grinned.

There was a loud pop from the wall behind Cale, and he turned fast enough to see blue sparks shoot out of the local station-environment box.

"Uh-oh, here we go again! Hang on!"

Cale grabbed the table, fast, and Tek did the same. Like everything else, the maintenance on environmental controls left something to be desired on Tau-14. Fortunately, life support and heat were in pretty good shape, but occasionally the G-enhancer would go out.

This meant that the amplified weights of everyone in the area controlled by the local G-enhancer would suddenly be reduced to their natural—on the asteroid—almost weightless, state.

If you weren't sitting down and hanging on, this could be very, uh, uplifting—

Suddenly the gravity ceased.

Aliens who had been walking between tables tumbled into the air, caught unprepared for their sudden light weight. The G-enhancer from the floor above caught a few and pulled them up, along with various bits of food, dishes, and even old scraps from the floor.

A noodle floated by Cale's mouth and he sucked it in—*sliiiip*—

He and Tek had been through this so many times he'd lost track.

Some wit had christened the local environmental control "Gravity Drive" in big bold letters. Had to be Human, too, since Cale could read it. Alien script was usually too hard to follow. Gravity Drive, that was funny.

Cale waited for the predictable end to the drama.

Yep.

Here came Cook, scuttling along the wall. He was wearing a small set of magnetic grippers. Shoes wouldn't have really been accurate, given the number and size of his locomotive feelers.

"Hold on everybody! I got it! I got it! Don't panic! Two seconds everybody! Calm, calm."

Cook gave a grunt as he smashed a feeler down on the environmental box.

"—ruuh, calm *down*—"

There was another blue spark and suddenly aliens dropped from the ceiling everywhere. Some of them hit pretty hard. A couple landed in other diners' plates.

"We gotta get out of this dump, Tek."

In front of him his plate plopped down, followed by his ET meatballs. The jolt woke the rest of the supposedly cooked critters up.

Zip-zip-zipzipzipzipzip—!

There they went, all heading in different directions. One lousy one left, and it was wiggling, stuck in the goop, but trying gamely to escape.

I am outta *here. Somehow, some way, I have got to get off this rock!*

Maybe he could go see what was up with that new ship. Might be that the beautiful pilot would like to be shown around a bit.

Yeah. And maybe they'd make him King of the Galaxy and hand him the keys to the station.

"I'm done, Tek, see ya later."

And Cale was off.

Cale stepped out of the commissary already planning how he'd introduce himself to the woman he'd introduce himself to the woman he'd seen earlier.

Hi there, my name's Cale, would you like to see the station?

Naw. Too simple.

How about, *What's a beautiful woman like you doing on a dump like this?*

No, that wasn't too good an idea, because then she might ask *him* what *he* was doing here, and being a rock-jockey wouldn't impress anybody, certainly not a pilot.

Hmm. Maybe he could just come right out and tell her she was the most beautiful thing he had ever seen and could he just follow her around and kiss the ground she'd walked on?

He was so deep in thought he actually didn't see the two aliens waiting for him down the hall until one of them reached out and pushed him back a step.

Huh?

It was Firrikash, the alien he'd bumped when he had tried to make the elevator.

And with him was his not-too-bright buddy, Po. Po was big, by Human or nonhuman standards. And mean, too. Neither alien was known for his love of Humans.

Oh, crap.

"Heyyy, Caille," said Firrikash.

"Ah, hey, Firrikash, Po. How they floatin'?"

"We keep hearrrring thingsssss," said Po.

"Abbbbout your *atti*tudde," added Firrikash.

He was in trouble here. "Huh! Is that so? Well, I guess I'll have to work on that—"

He started to back up, but he wasn't fast enough. Po reached out and smashed Cale across the side of his face. Cale went down.

"Ow!"

Yep, no doubt about it, he was in trouble here.

He started to get up.

All of a sudden there was a whistling sound and the two aliens let out yells as something grabbed their feet and pulled them over.

Cale looked down and saw a mesh chain wrapped around the nonhumans feet. A big Human stepped forward and began wrapping the other end of the mesh around their upper limbs. The man looked down at the two aliens and hit them.

They groaned.

"You wanna hunt Humans, you ought to remember we sometimes travel in packs."

He looked tough, but Cale was still angry.

"What are you *doing*?"

"Well, it's commonly known as helping," said the man.

"Yeah, well, what *for*?"

"Sometimes, kid, people just help each other out. For no particular reason."

"Oh, *right*. So you don't want anything in return for this help?"

"Well, actually I do."

There's solidarity for you, Tek.

Cale waited.

"I want you to risk your life. I want you to give up everything you have, leave everything you know, come with me, and face terror, torture, and possible death."

What was this guy on? Cale had known a few salvage workers who had flipped out after getting some bad depressants. He stole a glance to his right. He might make it up the hatch to Level 5 if he was fast.

"And I'd want to do all that *because* . . . ?"

"Because it's worth it. Because it might do some serious good."

Sure, it will. Might get you some good drugs if you sell my body to an organlegger. No, thanks.

He kept talking, as if he hadn't already said more than enough: "Because the Human race still matters, and you have a chance to prove it. And if that isn't good enough for you, then you're not man enough to handle this mission."

He's seriously off the deep end. Did this pervo really expect Cale to run off on some stupid *quest* with him?

"Gee, I never thought of it that way. I guess I've been wrong all these years, and it took your inspiring speech to make me see it. You've really changed me. Gosh, it's so . . . beautiful."

Cale looked up at the stranger.

"I think we gotta hug."

The man shook his head. "Geez, they've really ground you down, haven't they, kid?"

This was the last thing Cale wanted to hear. Who the hell was this guy to come in and tell him *he* was ground down?

"Listen, pal. Get this straight. I don't know you, I don't like you, and I don't want any part of your 'mission.' And I don't need your help with these morons."

Cale kicked Firrikash, who groaned.

"Okay, kid, your call."

And the guy reached down and popped the catch holding the chain shut.

Po and Firrikash cleared the chain and came to their feet grinning.

"I think the gentleman called you morons, boys. You know what that means? It's a particularly stupid kind of human."

Oh, man! Some kind of day today, all right. Get outta here, fast!

Cale didn't wait for the moron's hindbrains to kick it, he turned and ran like hell for the hatch to Level 5.

Po and Firrikash figured it out and lumbered after him.

Great. Just freakin' great!

— 5 —

Akima waited in the *Valkyrie*'s cockpit, already feeling as if her razor edge was starting to go dull. It
didn't take long when you were sitting in dock to get
itchy.

Hurry up, Korso, I want to fly!

It was only about ten minutes since they had docked,
but the prospect of an almost immediate liftoff raised
her spirits.

In her early training as a pilot, Akima noticed that the
rest of her life seemed pale compared to the time she
spent flying. She'd mentioned this once to her instructor.

Porter, a crusty old flier who'd piloted one of the ships
away from Earth, had smiled and looked straight at her,
a disconcerting move since Porter tended to talk, past
people, looking to the left or right of them.

"Honey, it ain't the rest of your life that's so bad, it's
that flyin' is so damn *good*."

Akima was startled to realize the truth of her words.

So even though she knew it was subjective, the relatively few minutes since the *Valkyrie* had docked had

stretched out and had already started to get boring.

Keeping a ship hot took only a small amount of skill. She engaged the autorefuelers from the station and charged the compressed air chambers. The *Valkyrie* was carrying enough reaction mass to fly halfway across the galaxy, so she didn't have to worry about the warp drive.

Akima checked the status of the in-system drives, as well as all the other systems.

Stith commed her during the weapons check.

"Hey, pilot, why looking at my teeth?"

"Just making sure they're sharp."

The Mantrin curled the edges of her beak up, an expression Akima knew was a smile.

"Maybe it's because you're a female of your species you are so . . . maternal."

"You know by now I'm full of care, Stith. Is that a redline in your second pulse bank?"

She reacted to that one, her head swiveling to the left as she checked her heads up display.

Made you look.

"Not bad, Akima. Now if you could only find me something to shoot, my life would be joyous."

Time to kill, got time to kill here.

Akima slid over to the navigation console and called up the logbook. She toggled the vox command on and gave the current stats on their expended energy, distance traveled, and current reaction efficiency.

Then, because she was bored, she told the computer to play back the logs for the previous several flights.

The last pilot, Djawana, had been a bit of a chatterbox. She added many colorful comments about the nature of their contacts on the previous three rocks Korso had taken them to.

On an asteroid called Sempa 5, Djawana had read the

stats for their flight, and then added, "The idiot running the dock here is so stupid he wouldn't even know the *Titan* if I tried to dock it. Which I guess I might if we find it."

What?

The Titan*? Is Korso looking for the* Titan*?*

Whoa. The *Titan* was the stuff of legends.

Of course, no one officially knew anything. The Human authorities had denied its existence since the destruction of Earth.

But on that day fifteen years ago, when a huge ship, the last off of Earth, had shot past thousands of fleeing ships, it had been *seen*. It's RF signature had been pulled, too, by several of the fleeing ships, including that of Akima's flight instructor.

"Oh, it was real, all right," Porter had told her, "and I never wanted anything so bad as to be at her controls."

A ship that fast and powerful—

That would be some ride.

But the ship had vanished, and no one had ever heard from it again. Sure, there was the odd, flaky freighter pilot who claimed he'd seen it from time to time—*Titan* sightings were part of modern mythology. And there were the rumors that someday the advanced ship would come back and save all of Humanity.

Yeah. Right.

But Korso and his crew seemed pretty tapped in. If they were looking for it, there was probably a good chance it was out there.

Of course, if Korso is looking for the Titan*, he'll need a pilot for it.* . . . Akima smiled. Things were getting better and better. It sure looked like this job was the best piece of luck she'd had in—well, in ever.

But if Korso *was* looking for the mythical ship, why hadn't he told her?

•   •   •

Lost in thought, she missed the first beep from the system proximity alarm she'd set. Any ship popping into the Tau-14 system would be picked up by the *Valkyrie*'s long range sensors, which would then alert her.

What the hell?

Three ships, and the sensors weren't coming up with a reading that she was familiar with.

Let's see.

She ran a check for RF. Zip. So much for passive.

The active sensors came up with more. The incoming trio of ships were big, two to three times the size of the *Valkyrie*, on a heading to Tau-14, bracketing the little asteroid. Their headings would hold the V-formation they were in, putting them in a triangle around the docking station.

Hmm. Now why would they want to do that?

There weren't any docked ships on Tau-14 except the *Valkyrie*.

Uh-oh.

The passive systems kicked in with an energy reading the likes of which she'd never seen.

Akima commed Gune. She hated to ask, but ship safety won over pride every time in her book.

"Hey, Gune, I hate to bother your nano-thing experiment and all, but I've got three unidentified ship types closing on Tau-14, and I was wondering if you'd seen this kind of energy profile before."

Gune nodded slightly and glanced to the right, where the ship's sensors were being routed to his station.

"Oh, yes, I know them. They're Drej."

Drej? Good God! Drej!

Gune didn't seem alarmed though, and continued with his description as though he were at a conference about strange and unusual spaceships.

"What they call their *Praojeh* class. Each one is well armed with coherent light weapons unique to the Drej and carries fifteen *slijah*. Er—what Humans call stingers."

"Thanks Gune—I'll get back to you."

Fifteen stingers each. That makes forty-five.

Plus the three launch ships.

Their gunner, Stith, seemed competent, but she doubted she was *that* good. If it came down to it, they would have to run.

The formerly cool pilot's chair seemed a little warmer now. Akima could feel a fine sweat on her forehead.

She commed Korso.

"Korso here."

"Captain, this is Akima."

She paused as she considered what to say next. Could the Drej intercept RF traffic?

"We're not alone."

Korso was sharp. "Good company?"

Akima glanced over to the kleersteel portal she'd reopened.

"That's a negative, Captain. I think we've fallen in with a very *bad* crowd."

Korso paused a second. "Copy that," he said. "Prep for departure while I get the package."

And then Akima thought she heard him mutter, "If the package is still in one piece."

Akima turned to her consoles. Since she'd kept the ship hot, the incoming ships wouldn't be able to see any sudden increases in the *Valkyrie*'s energy profile. They could launch at any time once Korso got back.

She ran through what little she'd managed to hear over the years about Drej tactics. There wasn't a lot, because the Drej were tough, and the tactics that didn't work against them were never passed on.

She recalled a speaker at the advanced flying class she'd taken. His name had been Healy, and he'd been up against the Drej in the original fight to save Earth. He still wore his Global Defense Force major's insignia tacked to his flight jumpsuit.

The subject for the day had been tactics. Healy had summed up all his successful fights with the Drej at the end of the session.

"The Drej are smart, fast, and efficient flyers. You've got to be smarter, faster, and more efficient to beat 'em."

The statement had always stuck with Akima as a way to live her entire life: smarter, faster, and more efficient than the next person. But now she wished Healy had been a bit more explicit with his help. Something like, "You hit the right hand pod, and they'll blow up every time."

No such luck.

How could she be more efficient?

Akima studied the formation the Drej were in around the station. They were in a roughly equilateral triangle surrounding the docking bay and outdoor docking arms. Nothing could leave the station without crossing all three ships' main guns.

One of the ships launched a corvette that docked across the way from the *Valkyrie*.

Akima studied each ship's position relative to her own and thought about how to use that knowledge.

As she considered, she kept checking the ship's status readouts. She paid extra attention to the in-system drive. If they had to make a run for it, they'd have to get to the warp boundary for the system before they could trigger the warp core and get away.

Everything looked good.

Come on Korso, let's get out *of here.*

Stith commed her, and seemed satisfied that they

would be leaving soon. Stith knew about the Drej, of course. "I stand ready," she said before discomming. "I can only hope they attack."

There was a ping signaling entry to the cockpit and Akima turned, hoping to see Korso.

But it was Preed. The alien gave her a stare that made her reevaluate her earlier conclusions about the carnal desires of all the crew members.

Eugh.

Just the *thought* of Preed after her made Akima's skin crawl.

"Yeah?" she said, staring right back at him.

"Captain Korso will not be entering the ship via the docking ring," said Preed. "He will, instead, rendezvous with us away from the asteroid."

"You sure?" asked Akima, The last thing she wanted was a stranded, pissed-off captain on her record.

"Quite," said Preed, "I tried to reach him on-station, but several Drej and he seemed to have gotten into a . . . disagreement. Our falling-back plan was to meet away from here. Since I am second in command, let's go."

Fine with me, thought Akima.

She commed Gune and Stith.

"We're getting out of here, kids," she said, "be ready for the worst."

A quick toggle and the clamps were disengaged. As Akima triggered the compressed gas, she thought she saw several black silhouettes standing in the docking ring staring at the *Valkyrie*.

Not a moment too soon, either.

The *Valkyrie* rose from under the docking clamps and shot toward the nearest Drej ship.

Akima had considered how to beat a smart, lightning-fast race. Position, she had concluded, was everything. Her angle of flight took her directly between two of the Drej ships. When both fired on the *Valkyrie*, they realized that they were also firing at each other.

Minor damage was done to both vessels before they stopped firing.

Akima felt like cheering. *Yes!*

The *Valkyrie*, with its powerful weapons, was not under any such limitation, and Akima could hear Stith cackling as she blasted away at both larger ships.

And then she saw on her viewscreen dozens of stingers forming up and coming toward them.

With only three ships, Akima could play the angles, but with another forty or so stingers on the way, this was not an option.

"Uh-oh."

Time was running out.

— 6 —

Cale ran down the corridor, Po and Firrikash right on his butt. "Gonna gettt you monkey boyyyy!" one of the two shouted at him.

Cale didn't bother to reply.

Oh, man, this is not *good at all.*

The two aliens were taller than him, with longer strides, and thus had a tendency to gain on the long stretches of corridor—like this one. Hmm. If he could get to one of the minihubs, he might be able to cut some corners.

There was one not far ahead. Looked like some work was being done on the roof wiring. It gave him an idea.

He risked a glance over his shoulder. They were about ten feet behind him. Not enough.

Cale dug in and sprinted.

He heard another cry from behind him, but he was into the minihub. He cut quickly to his right.

I may be slower than you on the long stretches, but you can't match my corners!

Bam—Cale slapped the wall and was heading almost

back the way he had come, but along a different corridor. He was right. Although the maintenance on the station's corridors was infrequent, it was consistent. Whenever a minihub's roof wiring was worked on, it was a safe bet that all the corridors leading into it had some work being done as well. There was a ceiling panel open just ahead. All right, four steps, three, two—!

Cale jumped and grabbed a support, swung up into the area above the corridor. Within a second he was out of sight.

We monkey boys can climb.

He heard Po and Firrakash getting closer.

"Coulddddn'ttt have run thisssss wayyyy."

"I ssssaw him turnnn!"

"Yooouuu ssssseee hhhimm? Nooo. Becaussse yyoouu're hhhunching bliiinnd!"

Cale froze as the pair walked directly underneath him. Fortunately, both aliens must have been from relatively flat planets. It didn't occur to them to look up.

Cale waited a few extra minutes. Nothing.

Carefully he swung down and looked both ways. They weren't in sight. He headed away from the direction he'd seen the aliens walking.

Thanks to that perv who'd "helped" him, he was out of a job. He certainly couldn't go back to work *now*, not when Po and Firrikash *knew* where he would be. They'd pound him.

Thanks for ruining my life with your help, *jerko*.

It was a setback, that was sure. No job meant no money for the ship, and who knew how long he'd have to keep watching out for Po and Firrakash?

I think it's time to do some more work on The Escape.

He'd go let Tek know and then clear out for a while. It was too bad, he was probably going to miss meeting the girl from that new ship.

Better than meeting her minus an arm or something.
Cale headed back to meet Tek.

As Cale walked through the doorway to the dining hall,
he saw Tek where he had left him. And—
Wasted metal, it's that perv!
Cale moved toward them quickly. Time to give this
guy a verbal. He wasn't going to have this jerko messing
with Tek.
"Hey! You still bothering people? Jet off, pal. My
buddy Tek doesn't want to go with you, either."
To Tek, Cale said, "I think I may have to lie low for
a while."
The perv smirked. "You don't know the half of it,
kid."
Didn't this guy get the hint? What was it going to
take? Should he thump him?
Hmm. Let's not forget the guy'd flattened both Po *and*
Firrikash. Probably not smart to push him too hard.
"How about you just get out of here, okay? Leave us
be."
"Great job with the kid, Tek. He's a real charmer."
Huh?
Tek laughed. "I had expected you to take him off my
hands a lot sooner. What do you want from an old blind
person?"
"Tek, you *know* this guy?"
The big man smiled. "Name's Joseph Korso. I was
with your father on the *Titan* project."
Cale glared at Korso. "I don't *have* a father." Then to
Tek. "Did you bring this guy here?"
"More or less."
"I don't get it. Why?"
Korso leaned forward and put his hand on Cale's
shoulder.

"Do you still have that ring your father gave you?"

Cale nodded, twisting to get Korso's hand off him. "Watch the weave, pal." *What does that old ring have to do with anything?*

"Give it here. The ring."

Cale stared at the man. *Give it to* him? *Who did this bloober think he was,* give *it to* him—?

Tek said, "Go ahead. It's all right."

Cale frowned, but he reached under his shirt and pulled out a chain. The ring, long since too small for his finger, hung on the chain.

Korso reached out and grabbed the ring, tugging back *hard*. The chain dug into Cale's neck and then snapped—*ping!*

"Hey! What the hell are you *doing*—?"

And then he stopped, fascinated. Korso *did* something. The ring seemed to . . . *segment* somehow, while staying together.

Cale had never seen it do anything like *that*.

Korso began pushing the segments in a sequence, one, two—Cale lost track.

This went on for a few seconds, and then the ring *beeped*.

Korso grunted and held the ring out to Cale. It seemed to be *glowing*. And it was bigger around than it had been, too.

"Put it on."

Cale stared at the ring.

Oh, man, this day is getting stranger and stranger all the time.

"Tek . . . ?"

"Go ahead, Cale. It's all right."

"C'mon, kid, we're in kind of a hurry here."

"Not me. I'm retired, I got all day."

Tek said, "Cale . . ."

He mentally shrugged. What the hell. He slipped the ring onto his finger. It fit just fine.

Well, whoop-de-do. Guy comes all the way from God knows where to resize my dad's ring for me. Big deal—

The ring lit up like a flashlight.

Hello?

Tiny circuits glowed as the ring become transluscent. A thin silver stream of glowing light began to move *out* of the ring. Nanomachines? The streams *flowed* down his finger and onto his palm.

Cale held his hand up to watch more closely as the stream began to take on a pattern. It was gorgeous, a filigreed web of intersecting points, lines, and whorls.

What the hell was it?

"It's a map," Korso said, answering his unanswered question. "The ring is a storage device, genetically encrypted to your father—and you. It won't work for anyone else."

A map?

Korso continued. "Your father's last mission was to hide the *Titan* where the Drej couldn't find it. To hide it where *nobody* could find it. Nobody except you."

"That ship means everything, Cale," said Tek. "Humanity's future depends on you finding it. You see, you *do* have a future."

"Me? Whoa, whoa, *whoa*. Not *me*. Tek *listen*—not *me*. I've got other plans, not this . . ."

Tek shook his head slightly. "It's time to stop running, Cale. You're Human—and you *can* make a difference."

"Actually, I think maybe we should start running." Korso's voice had a funny edge to it. "Now."

Cale looked over at the doorway where Korso was staring.

Two Drej drones stood in the doorway.

"Told you we were in a hurry."

Cale had seen all manner of aliens in his life, some of them pretty creepy looking, but the Drej still took the prize. They were the spookiest creatures he had ever seen. Their bodies were almost black; tall, skeletal structures with joints that were distinctly alien. A kind of inner light glowed under the dark skin, and this sickly radiance *pulsed* to some kind of internal beat.

Brrr. The effect gave him a chill.

The Drej had elongated fingers gripping equally evil-looking weapons. At first glance, the guns seemed to have no power units, but Cale knew that the laser's power inputs were attached directly to the upper bodies of the Drej. One of the creatures had its mouth open, and the interior was . . . pitch black.

Lord, Lord. "What do *they* want?"

"They want *you*, kid, for the same reason I do. Only, they'd just as soon you were *dead*."

Cale shook his head. "Dead? How do you know that—?"

The Drej scanned the room, their heads moving in jerky stop-motion. They twitched, like a small animal Cale had seen in a documentary about Earth. What was it—Swirl? Skirl? *Squirrel*, that was it. Big, black, glow-in-the-dark, ugly squirrels—

And now they looked right at *him*.

Their weapons came up.

Oh, *man!* "Okay, okay—I'm convinced!"

Cale dove to the deck, grabbing Tek as he did so. Laser fire flashed overhead, Korso pried the table up, turned it on its side, then ducked behind it, returning fire. His weapon—some kind of slug thrower?—seemed to *splash* off of something in front of the Drej. The Drej weren't hurt, but rocked back somewhat.

Some kind of shield?

All around them, aliens and humans screamed, cried, and ducked for cover.

"We gotta get to the kitchen!" Korso yelled.

Cale looked around the commissary. Not an easy way to go. The kitchen entrance was all the way across the room. They had to make it all the way over there in front of two hunching Drej, firing *lasers*. They'd be like targets in a computer shooting gallery!

Tek motioned to Cale. He lifted his arms and flapped them around. Had Tek been hit? Why wasn't he saying anything? He was blind, not *mute*.

Then Cale understood.

The environmental control box!

"Got it!" he said.

"Korso! Over there—the box marked 'gravity drive'!"

Korso frowned, then Cale saw him understand.

Korso fired, his weapon's missile easily piercing the casing on the environmental control box.

As had happened before, humans and aliens went flying. The Drej, caught unprepared, started that way as well.

Korso fired another few shots at them. This time his weapon seemed to be doing some damage.

Guess their shields aren't spherical, Cale had time to think.

Korso was pushed back a bit by the force of his weapon, but he'd locked his feet under a table, so he didn't go far.

"You ready, kid?"

Cale grabbed Tek's shoulder. "Come on, Tek, I'll lead you in."

"I'll stay here," Tek said.

"You can't! You'll get fried!"

A burst of fire came from the Drej. They seemed to be recovering from their new positions near the roof.

A chair exploded nearby, pieces just missing Cale. "Whoa!"

"Take care of him, Korso."

Cale was torn. Tek *had* to come. "No, no, no—you're coming!"

Tek shook his head. Cale looked at his mentor and knew he was right. Tek wouldn't make it to the kitchen.

But maybe if the Drej wanted *him*, maybe they wouldn't bother Tek once he was gone. . . .

"Go, Cale. I'll read about you."

Korso fired at the Drej, hit one, and spun it like a toy. "Let's go, kid. Move! Follow me."

Korso pulled his feet loose, twisted, and fired his gun at the wall opposite the kitchen and used the reaction to propel him toward the kitchen. It was an effective move—he zipped back there fast enough, although the landing obviously wasn't as well-planned.

Cale heard a crashing of pots and pans and a few curses. The environmental controls seemed to be fine in the kitchen.

Time to go.

"Good-bye, Tek," he said softly.

The Drej were starting to recover again, so Cale took another table and braced himself on the wall before shoving it toward them, using his salvage skills to arc the huge metal rectangle directly at them.

The table slammed into them, hard.

Bad catch, boys. You won't make any salvage points that way.

Cale pushed off and flipped, landed on his feet, upside down on the ceiling. The environmental control from the level above gave him enough weight to keep moving.

Lucky the Drej hadn't figured that out yet.

But the Drej weren't stupid, and Cale could see them reorienting themselves as he ran toward the kitchen. He made it about three quarters of the way across the room before the firing started again.

Uh-oh. Cale dived off the roof, tucked, and flipped, arcing for the kitchen.

He heard Korso fire and then he was in.

—*Thump*!

Made it.

Yeah, made it to the *kitchen.*

The question was, what now?

— 7 —

Cale watched Korso fire his weapon under the double, swinging doors of the kitchen entrance. There was nothing for a second, then the Drej replied with an almost continuous burst of laser fire. Smoke boiled from the walls and reflected heat strobed him.

Cale took a fast look around the dingy, smelly kitchen. Pots and pans lay everywhere, and strange-looking stains ran down the wall. In the corner, a few of the uncooked meatballs scurried about. There was a smell, too, worse than lunch.

Maybe it's dinner.

There came a hissing sound.

Now what?

Opposite the door, sparks erupted from the wall—a plasma torch. Since the Drej didn't need a plasma torch, that meant someone else was cutting their way in.

Great. Now we have the station cops after us.

To add to the excitement, from somewhere, Cook started babbling, "Oh, my *food*! You are *terrible*! You guys are . . . are . . . *unsanitary*!"

Cale looked up. There Cook was, perched on a bar on the ceiling. He looked worried—if an alien insectoid could be said to look worried.

Right. As if Cook had any room to talk about unsanitary anything.

"When they catch you I'll *testify*, and you'll *never* get out of jail!"

Cale thought jail sounded pretty good about now. No Po, no Firrikash, and maybe no Drej trying to kill him.

Yeah, sure. The way this day is going, I'd wind up with them as cellmates.

A particularly nasty burst of laserfire raked the room, working its way toward the ceiling.

"Drej. I gotta go now," said Cook.

Go?

Cale watched as Cook scuttled over to an open vent and disappeared.

Korso had seen it, too. He motioned with a thumb. "Let's follow ugly, there."

Cale jumped up and grabbed the perch Cook had been on. He hauled himself over to the vent.

"Great idea. No one will ever think to look for us in the *vent*."

"If you have a better suggestion, kid, I'm listening."

Cale shrugged. Nothing came to mind.

They went.

The vent was dark and cramped. Ahead of them, Cale could see the cook moving along at a good rate, faster than he would have thought possible.

There was a commotion behind them, and Cale knew the kitchen was no longer empty.

Won't take a detective to figure out where we went, either.

He increased his crawl speed.

"Go! Go!" whispered Korso needlessly.

"I'm going!"

Ahead was a six-way intersection. Which way? Left, right, up, down, or straight?

Korso shoved Cale down.

Well, I guess we're going this *way.*

It wasn't a moment too soon, either, as a flash of laser light briefly illuminated the vent intersection where they had just been. Cale didn't have much time to see it, however, because he was too busy trying to slow his fall down the vent.

Yow!

Cale found reserves he hadn't known he had and managed to catch himself before he fell to the bottom of the station and into the air recyclers.

"You have any idea where we're going?" he asked Korso.

"Yes, I do."

They came to another intersection. There was a different smell to this one—kind of oily. Korso motioned and Cale moved into the oily-smelling passage.

They moved along for probably a hundred meters or so, and then Korso pointed to a grating ahead, in what was now the roof. "Time we got out of here," he said. "That way."

Cale shoved at the grating, but it didn't budge. Korso pushed him out of the way and manhandled the grate open. There was a loud clatter as the grating fell on the *floor* above. Gravity was all screwed up, and it took Cale a second to reorient himself as to which way down was. The two of them dropped from the vent.

They were in the old repair hanger.

Cale had been here hundreds of times "acquiring" parts for *The Escape.*

There were loads of old repair projects in the hangar.

Cale had once thought about renting a space here for his project, but had saved money by keeping it out on the asteroid.

They headed off toward the far doors.

Go through there and then we have any number of ways out.

There was a piercing whistle from somewhere.

Are we ever *going to catch some luck?*

They glanced around quickly. Behind them came a sound from the vent, and ahead, whistling merrily away were the station cops.

"Go! Go! Go!" shouted Korso.

Go? Go where*?*

Cale turned. The older man gestured toward a sleek-looking fighter parked nearby.

Well, at least Korso seemed to have some taste. The fighter was an old Akrennian ship, made for dual, atmospheric and space, flight. Cale had admired it before, but had never thought he'd be stealing it.

He jumped in ahead of Korso and started to check the flight console.

Korso leapt in after him. "Move over!"

"Hey, I can fly, too!"

"Not today, kid," said the man. "Maybe if you live until you're older."

Cale frowned. That had a familiar ring to it—

Korso flipped switches, activating the drive systems.

A laser beam splashed off the ceiling overhead, burned a black gouge into the hard plastic as the ship's canopy slid into place.

Cale turned to look for the Drej. Where were they?

"It won't start."

What?

Cale looked over at Korso, ready to tell the older man

to move over. Suddenly there came the hard press of acceleration.

"Got it!"

They shot toward the exterior airlock doors.

Unfortunately, the Drej had already begun closing off *that* route.

The ship spun as Korso hit the wheel brakes.

"Hey!"

"Hang on kid."

Hang on? To what*? Where were they going?*

"They've locked down the doors!"

Korso grinned.

"We're not going forward, we're going *up*."

Up?

Cale looked out through the top of the canopy and saw a huge kleerplas panel.

That goes into the main concourse!

It probably wasn't the safest way to design a space station, with skylights in all of the hangars, but Cale didn't really care at the moment.

They shot toward the panel. Closer, closer—

There was a clattering crash, and they were through. Aliens and humans shot to the left and right, dodging the falling fragments of kleerplas.

Korso held them there for a moment, hovering.

A laser splashed onto their dorsal wing—which didn't look too good right now. Probably this ship wasn't going to be making any atmospheric flights soon—

And they dove toward another kleerplas panel.

Looks like bay twelve. . . .

Yep. Cale made out the numbers after they smashed through the second panel. The impacts weren't doing the ship's nose any good, either.

No Drej in this bay, but somebody must have gotten smart. The vacdoors were closing. Usually they only did

that if the station had been holed by a meteor or something. There was no way they were going to smash
through *those.*

I bet they're doing that in all the hangars.

Cale gave Korso a look. *Well, genius, what now?*

Korso slammed the accelerator knob forward.

"Better brace yourself kid."

"Brace myself for *what*—? There was no *way* they
were going to make it to the end of hangar twelve before
the vacdoors shut. No frigging way! What the hell was
Korso thinking?

Cale's life, short though it was, began to play before
him. Yeah, well, it might not have been great, but it
hadn't been too bad a life, at least not so bad he wanted
to *leave* it yet—

What was Korso saying?

"Eject. Where's the Eject? Cale. *Cale!* This model
does have Eject, right?"

Instantly, Cale figured it out. Of course.

They were almost to the vacdoors when Cale leaned
forward and hit the Eject button.

The canopied portion of the ship immediately shot
forward, driven by explosive bolts that propelled their
section of the craft even faster.

They shot through the gap, barely missing the edges
of the vacdoors. Another coat of sealant and they
wouldn't have made it.

The rest of the ship wasn't so lucky. There was a huge
fireball behind them, and the blast caught them and
kicked them away even faster from the station.

Korso laughed. "And you were *worried.*"

Cale looked out through the canopy. Apparently the
explosion had done more than just move them away
from the station faster. A thin spiderweb of cracks began
to crawl across the kleerplas.

What was the pressure crack rule? Cale tried to remember.

Solid crack, might come back, web of cracks, twenty seconds max . . . ,

Cale glanced over. Now *Korso* was looking worried. He reached down and pulled a comm off his belt.

"Akima? Korso. We're requesting a pickup here . . ."

A voice came from the comm. A *female* voice.

"I'm right above you. Can you get to me?"

Cale thought. Could they maneuver the pod up into the hangar of the *Valkyrie* before the cracks shattered the dome? Could they maneuver the pod at all?

No and *no.*

"Not enough time," the older man said.

Korso reached down to a compartment by his feet. He came out with a fire extinguisher and grabbed Cale by the collar.

"Exhale."

Exhale? "You gotta be kidding."

The only reason Korso could want him to exhale—

"Exhale!"

"Oh, no! No—"

Korso sprayed Cale's face with the slimy foam from the extinguisher. Cale went blind, but he felt more of the foam cover him as the man kept spraying. A few seconds went past, Cale exhaled, spewing as much of his air out as he could—

There was a sudden tearing sound, and then the canopy either burst or was blasted out. Cale wasn't sure because he couldn't see. The gel from the extinguisher opaqued as it froze on his face.

Welcome to vacuum, he had time to think. *So, long, Cale—*

And then he blacked out.

• • •

Stiff. God he was stiff. What had he had to drink last night? Whatever it was, he was going to tell Tek to erase it from his rations card. He could hardly move.

There was a rasping voice. "Cale. Cale? You alive?"

Alive? Not much. Who was that? It sounded familiar. . . .

Korso. Korso? It wasn't a dream—

Cale decided to answer the voice. "Maybe," he managed, thinking how dry and croaky his *own* voice sounded. "My skin feels . . . weird."

"That's because your blood froze," answered the voice.

Yeah, sure. And he'd come back from the dead as well. "Oh. I guess that explains it." Blood froze. Shee-it, it had.

But that was all he had time to think before the world went black again.

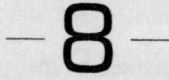

8

Akima allowed herself a moment of panic as she looked at the swarm of Drej stinger ships closing on the *Valkyrie*.

Good Gods, look at them all! And they want to kill me! What the hell am I supposed to do?

And then her years of training kicked in. The pilot took a deep breath and let it out. She took another, and relaxed the edges of her focus, doing her best to encompass *all* the viewscreens at once.

First on the agenda, better get some thinking distance.

She triggered the main thrusters, sliding the accelerator back to three-quarters of full. The acceleration pressed her head back into the pilot's chair, hard.

I may not be able to outmanuever you suckers, but I sure as hell can outrun you.

Akima swung the ship down from the ecliptic toward the south pole of the asteroid.

The main docking station was on the north pole so this put her well out of range of the three mother ships.

Gonna need some ideas here.

Her current strategy was working at the moment: the stingers following were behind the *Valkyrie* far enough to be easy targets. Stith and Preen could pot them like rats in a vat.

But she'd noticed that about half the stingers had broken off the attack as she'd headed down. That probably meant they were moving to intercept on the other side of the asteroid.

"Computer: Conference weapons, engineering, auxiliary gun 2."

Immediately, tiny versions of Stith, Preen, and Gune appeared off to her right.

"Okay, guys, way I figure it, when we get around to the other side, we'll be caught in a net. Any ideas?"

She turned the ship upside down, dodging a series of small missiles from one of the stingers.

"Blow the hell out of it, and we'll get away." Preen.

Stith seemed almost to glow. "Yesss. None of the stingers can take us singly, and our run-and-hit position is good. We will *devour* them."

Her beak opened and clacked together twice. *"Devour."*

"Go back how we came." Gune.

Now there was an idea. It would give them the element of surprise, and an unimpeded attack run on the larger ships back at the station.

The only problem was how to do it fast enough to be a surprise. Too slow and the following Drej would create a semi-sphere and the crossfire would destroy the *Valkyrie.*

Gotta get back to the dock—

Aha!

"Gune—I'm going to need you to crank up the oxy distillers."

Gune nodded. He'd already figured it out.

Guess it's pretty hard to surprise a genius.

Preen hadn't figured it out, though. "What are you planning, Human?"

"We're going back—but not how they expect. Get ready for some shakes. Oh, and deploy your hi-gee fields."

The hi-gee fields would reduce some of the effects of the acceleration she had planned, but not all. Akima thought she saw Preen glare a bit before she killed the visual—Akrennians hated hi-gee. Too bad. She was going to need zero distractions for this.

The trick was how to maintain surprise. Most spaceships couldn't fly the tight arcs and loops of an on-planet dogfight: there was no air to catch, and not much gravity to fight. So space dogfights tended to be long, slow parabolas—inertia and momentum were constants, after all.

This ought to surprise 'em.

Akima slowed down, taking the ship to half throttle, allowing the Drej to get closer. Not *too* close, or she'd risk more damage—

Then, as the Drej were almost on them, Akima killed the main drive.

"Human! Keep going!"—it was Preen.

Akima didn't pay any attention.

Shut up, baboon face.

Instantly she forced the full measure of air from the right front and left, rear docking jets. She watched three screens at once, along with a computer generated copy of the ship mapped near the original course.

The tiny copy was turning on its axis to face backward. Fast.

Momentum, momentum, now!

She triggered an equal amount of air from the left front and right, rear docking jets as the ship neared 180 degrees, then immediately fired the drive, full blast.

A drink she'd forgotten about shot to the back of the cockpit, clattering as it hit the bulkhead behind her.

There were several muted yells from Stith and Preen.

The *Valkyrie* shot forward—straight toward the on-coming Drej.

Akima allowed herself a smile as she flew toward the ships that had only moments before been pursuing them. Stingers split off in all directions out of the path of the *Valkyrie*.

It didn't do some of them much good. Stith and Preen were deadly gunners, and the forward battery took out two stingers as she watched. Red laser light reached out from the *Valkyrie* and pierced the black hulls of the ships. White explosions brightened the dark side of the asteroid as the small fighters vaporized. No sound, of course.

Mess with the best, die like the rest.

"Yes! Excellent work, Human! You have led us to rich hunting!"

Stith sounded ecstatic. Akima figured that the race's reputation in war was well deserved if the alien was any example.

"Gune, over-amp our oxy—I've got a feeling we're going to need it."

"Yes."

That Gune. Real big on the chatter.

Now that they had gotten surprise on their side, Akima wanted to keep it. But how?

They came up on the outskirts of the station. Below was one of the smelting furnaces for ship salvage. The pilot noticed a piece of salvage coming in low, phosphor markers flashing.

She checked a tally assigned to a subscreen. Of the

twenty-five or so stingers that had pursued the *Valkyrie* around the asteroid, there were only about a dozen left. If they could lose the rest before reaching the station, that would leave only about twenty more—plus the mother ships.

Well, that's being optimistic. Only *twenty?*

Akima didn't know for sure what Korso had in mind for an escape, but she'd bet a stack of goldstar credits that he'd need *some* kind of cover, which meant the *Valkyrie* needed to be back in the area. Anything that could reduce the odds against them was worth trying.

Yeah, if we survive.

She took a deep breath and kicked the *Valkyrie* toward the planetoid. The big ship skimmed a few meters above the pockmarked, ugly surface.

"Stith, Preen—whatever you do, don't fire at the salvage—"

"Freeze it, Human, we weren't born yesterday!"

"All right, great hunters, any ideas?"

"I shall undertake to shoot them all." This from Stith. "This would be the best solution."

"Oh, well, great. I feel *much* better. Listen, I'm going to be busy for a few minutes, so nobody distract me."

Akima lifted the ship up to about salvage height. Immediately her heads up display flashed red, followed by vocal warnings.

"Collision warning thirty degrees to port. Collision warning thirty degrees to starboard, Collision warning—"

The pilot killed audio warnings and checked the rear viewscreens. Behind them, like wolves closing on a deer, the stingers came on.

Excellent.

The trick now was to dodge the incoming salvage, and to lead the Drej into the way of it.

Akima didn't really think she could outmanuever the Drej, but if her memories of the cheap security on stations like this was accurate—

Yes!

Two trios of stingers came zooming up alongside the *Valkyrie*. They probably planned to board the larger ship.

The path of the *Valkyrie* at that moment was right between three well-traveled lines of salvage. To get alongside her meant that the aliens either had to move around the salvage, or to destroy it—

Which they did. And as the salvage became targets for the Drej, so did the stingers become targets themselves.

Tau-14, so cheap when safety was concerned, had placed a much higher priority on protecting its lifeblood of salvage materials. Hidden gunports from the surface of the station opened up and began taking out any ship firing on salvage.

The six ships vaporized. A few more were caught in the shrapnel and damaged enough so they wouldn't be following.

Akima grinned. She pulled up fast from the surface. No time to be mistaken as a problem by an automated security gun.

Just ahead lay the station.

Akima twisted the ship into a roll, dodging more Drej missiles as they approached the station. The situation still wasn't great, but it was better.

When the hell was Korso going to show up?

"Stith, you ready with our surprises?"

"Yes AK-IMMA. Three packages ready for delivery."

First time she's used my name. Guess I'm moving up in the world.

The pilot put the ship into a dive under one of the

docking arms. The Drej, now more than a bit wary about firing on the station, held their fire for a few moments.

In that time, Akima was within a few thousand meters of one of the mother ships.

Three pips sounded, indicating missiles had been launched. She flipped the ship using the docking jets and shot up, away from the asteroid.

"Akima, this is Korso. We're requesting a pickup here."

Akima put the direction finder on Korso's signal and zeroed in on the navscreen before flipping the ship yet again and diving back toward the asteroid.

Stith was singing some kind of deep voiced battle chant as the pilot reached visual on the Akrennian fighter cockpit Korso's signal was coming from.

The fighters were closing once more. Akima started to sweat again. They were so close to getting away with this—

Then one of the larger Drej ships blew up. There was a second explosion near another, and Preen let out a yip.

"It worked!"

Akima didn't bother to ask, but commed Korso again.

"I'm right above you. Can you get to me?"

The visual from Korso's signal wasn't too clear, but Akima thought he looked worried. He nodded in answer to her question. Behind the captain she could see the canopy of the fighter. Were those *cracks*? Korso wasn't wearing a pressure suit.

Uh-oh.

There wouldn't be time for a docking.

"Gune, overpressurize bay one. Try a three or four X and be ready to blow it on my signal."

This was going to be tight.

"Stith, Preen, keep 'em off my back for a few more seconds."

"Of course," Stith said. "Come to Stith, fools!"

Akima moved the *Valkyrie* as close to the top of the fighter as she could and lined it up with docking bay one. She got a camera visual on the canopy. Here came Korso's foot—

"Gune, blow it—*Now!*"

Akima dropped the *Valkyrie* even closer to the cockpit.

Good luck, boss.

She saw a brief glimpse on her subscreen as two men popped out of the escape cockpit, and then her sensors showed them in bay one.

Akima reached for the button that would repressurize the bay, but Gune had beaten her to it. There. Mission accomplished.

Let's skip this system.

The pilot picked the direction with the fewest Drej between her and open space and hit the throttle. She spared a thought for Korso and his package and held off the higher acceleration. Ten stingers followed her out into space.

"Akima, this is Gune. I have the captain and his cargo safely in the medic bay."

Well, that's my cue—

Akima rammed the throttle forward and felt the snap as the acceleration drove her into her seat. The stingers began to recede.

So long, suckers.

– 9 –

Susquehana stood in the Making chamber and considered the needs of the Drej race. The Orb would keep her from choosing a path too unbalanced, but the main analysis was hers.

Ali heben ne kipor quan id. Heavy is the burden on the Queen's head.

She considered: The ship needed more care than the previous Making. The *Alahenena*'s power source was not yet under control, and the current estimates had the makeshift white-dwarf shields failing an alarming five percent more than it had before. This indicated an exponential trend.

Not good.

This would seem to call for more worker-class *droheh* to repair the failing shields, or, at the least, to prepare another layer of the makeshift shield. On the other limb, more *droheh* might be able to calculate a better way of arranging the shield materials.

And more droheh are more possible enemies to worry about.

*YOUR CHOICE WILL BE FREE FROM PER-
SONAL GAIN*

Of course it would. The Orb needed not remind her.
There would be the necessary numbers of *droheh*. The
high-level brains of the *droheh* would serve to keep her
sharpened; the race could ill afford a dull Queen.

Deeheh were needed to keep the Drej battle strength
up as well. Since her ingestion of the Orb there had been
no new conquests to add to the Drej worlds. Existing
conquests had been maintained, of course, but perhaps
this was the period she could begin to expand. . . .

The thought of altering the proportion of the Making
toward mainly *deeheh* was such a pleasant one. Imagine
the power!

No. There needed to be a better balance—this time.
With the search for the *Titan* in progress as well, she
might be able to justify a few more points of *deeheh*,
but not the inspiring *quata* she wished.

The search, of course, would require more *daiheh*.
Drej pilots were specialized, and there were few of any
race who could match their intuitive understanding of
space.

Numbers began to coalesce in the Queen's head. Per-
centages of *droheh, daiheh, deeheh, and douheh* altered,
changed. Each drone type required certain modifications
and subgroupings: Some *deeheh* were attackers; some
scouts. There were *daiheh* who were needed for ground
transport, *droheh* who could fight, and even *douheh* with
high-level cognitive abilities.

The numbers shifted—more toward creative tasks, a
shade less toward destructive ones.

Yes.

CONCUR

The Orb agreed with her assessment. The Making
could begin.

• • • •

The queen allowed herself a few moments to check the Making room. There had never been a succession before or just after a Making—the process of lifegiving was sacred to the Drej—but it was prudent to be careful.

Where there is weakness, one will exploit it.

Wise words from a predecessor—one who had survived a thousand Makings.

Having confirmed that there was no danger, Susquehana summoned the power of the Orb and linked to *Lanoor* the life-giving Artifact.

Matrices were drawn from the Orb and combined into the permutations described by the Queen's earlier analysis. She tilted back her head and called forth the power.

The power.

The power to bring forth Drej.

Makings were not physically restricted to any particular time period—the *Lanoor* could make Drej at any time. The tradition, however, was to keep Makings spaced out by one cycle—the original annual period of the Drej home world. The Drej prided themselves on efficiency, and it was one further test of a Queen's competency to accurately foresee the labor needs of the race.

Susquehana felt the power coursing through her being. The tools were ready. Now she needed materials.

She marshaled the power of the Orb and opened the iris of the gathering lens. Fiber-optic cables linked to thousands of points on the hull of the *Alahenena* gathered the light from stars and distant galaxies. The mixed result, the pure light of the heavens, shone down on Susquehana.

I call you forth.

Using the power of the Orb, the Queen took the light and channeled it into the translucent floor of the Making chamber. Thousands of pools of light began to take shape across the vast chamber.

I give you form.

The pools began to glow brighter, taking on the shapes of various drone types. There were all sizes of drone, from the smallest scout to the largest fighter. Susquehana's mind, immensely powerful, strained with the effort to ingrain each of the thousands of drones-to-be with their new classifications and abilities.

As each form matured into a final state, the light within appeared to dim. The fleshy envelopes of the drone's bodies hid the intense fires of their creation.

I give you purpose.

Susquehana used the Orb to send thoughts to the *Drej* embryos before her. The Orb sent a history of their race while she sent them the intangible feeling of what it was to *be* Drej.

You are your own, you are individual.

None of the previous Queens had been able to explain why this part worked, nor could the Orb. Somehow the drones she had created were about to become sentient, to gather their own spark from somewhere.

We are Drej.

And the ceremony was done.

As she had twice before, Susquehana felt a combination of exhaustion and exhilaration. She surveyed the ten thousand new Drej and considered how fortunate she was to have become Queen.

To know this power, this creation, is to truly know what it is to be Drej.

"Go to your places."

The Drej began to leave the chamber, pouring out into the ship. Some would leave the ship on transports, bound for Drej conquests or outlying bases. The vast majority, however, would stay here, on the *Alahenena*, the largest concentration of her people in the galaxy.

The Queen cloaked herself and waited for the chamber to empty. No point in leaving the route of temptation for her new subjects. It would truly be foolish for the new Drej to attack her now, of course, but why leave the route open?

As the last of the newly made Drej left the Making chamber, the Queen was contacted.

It was Fantiquar, the new leader of the communications section. Susquehana closed the portal of the Making chamber and sent a projection to the communications center. The spherical projection resembled herself as viewed in an Orb-like shape and was capable of receiving sensory input as if she occupied its very place. Since even she could not be in every location at once, her projections were useful and necessary tools for leading effectively.

And they do not put me at risk.

Privately she thought that whoever had first used the Orb to create projections must have been thinking along those very lines.

Far away, in the communications section, her projection spoke.

"Report."

"My Queen. News comes regarding your search for the human biobod ship."

The *Titan*!

Fantiquar continued with the report.

As he spoke, a channel for visual data was opened and a stream of images began to appear as a layer in his communication.

Susquehana saw the squalid interior of a human feeding chamber. Ugly biobods milled about, some seated at long, troughlike surfaces, their heads low over containers of some kind of biomatter. The very thought of ingesting biomatter was disgusting in the extreme and had always seemed to be a matter that biobods would want to do privately. As far as the Queen was concerned, it was just one further indication of their perversity that they chose to consume it in front of one another. One of the biobods reached out as part of its food attempted to escape.

They are eating it alive. Disgusting.

"Is there a purpose to this . . . scene?"

"Yes my Queen. Notice—"

The images froze. Susquehana noticed a *deeheh* to the right of viewpoint and realized that the data had been collected from a Drej. She noted the identification signature of the data collector and opened another channel as she listened to Fantiquar's report.

The current status of the Drej who had collected the feeding chamber data was difficult to make out. It seemed to be crawling along a tight, dark corridor, using a focus burner to clear the area ahead of it.

Susquehana identified other Drej in the area and did a survey of their viewpoints. Nothing interesting inside.

From shipviews outside the biobod station, which she now understood was known as 'Tau-14' she watched as an Earth-made ship shot over the horizon. Whoever was commanding was alert and immediately launched fighters.

Susquehana allowed her focus to shift back to Fantiquar as he completed his phrase. "—here."

A portion of the image from the feeding chamber became highlighted. A young Human sat in the corner of the room.

"We have identified this young Human as Cale Tucker."

Cale Tucker!

The offspring of the designer of the *Titan*.

Well, here was excellent news.

"Note, my Queen, the human's hand."

The hand of the young human enlarged to fill the data stream. With Drej perception as clear as it was, there was no loss of clarity as the hand grew. Immediately Susquehana noted a silvery glow on the biobod's appendage. It resembled something familiar.

A star map!

So it was true. There had been rumors of a map among the humans for years, but none had ever checked out. The human, unfortunately, had not held his hand in such a way that the entire map was visible, but there seemed to be quite a bit.

Susquehana checked the viewpoints available on Tau-14. There was chaos on the station, but no Cale Tucker in sight. A time lapse view of the moments since her earlier check indicated that the young human had fled the station. Exterior station views showed that a number of the fighters launched after the Earth ship were missing. The Queen watched a current viewpoint. The Earth ship was ahead of a group of *slijah* and seemed to leap ahead, accelerating.

Then it vanished, a spectrum-hued warp Artifact in its wake.

He is gone!

The Mother Drej allowed herself a private moment of anger. There was no way she could have been contacted any earlier with the news, however. Makings were not interruptible, by their very nature.

Fantiquar would survive this day.

"You have performed well," she acknowledged. "Contact the ships surrounding Tau-14 and have them begin a warp signal trace. Immediately."

If Fantiquar was surprised that she knew the name of the asteroid, he gave no sign.

Susquehana contacted the main *daiheh* for *Alahenena*. "Prepare us for transport."

Between the glimpse of the map and the warp trace, they would track the Earth ship and find Cale Tucker.

Who knew? Perhaps the humans had had enough time to analyze the map and were even now jumping to where the *Titan* lay.

If so, the Drej would have it soon.

It was well. Events were moving better than she could have planned them.

—10—

There was a face above Cale. It was gorgeous, an angel's face. A *female* angel's face. It stirred certain parts of him, and it seemed vaguely familiar.

Wait a second here. It was—the pilot!

Suddenly, a horrible face replaced the beautiful one. Fangs gleamed in a mouth set below an alien set of eyes. Metal bits made up part of the creature's misshapen skull. Ugly squared.

Ugly spoke. "Is it dead? Can we *eat* it?"

"No, *it* is *not* dead! Who are you? Get away from me!"

What the hell was going on? Cale tried to remember. He'd been at work, it had started off as such a nice day. And then he'd gone to lunch. Something *bad* had happened then.

As he tried to remember, the two faces moved about over him. Cale tried to move, and realized he was strapped to some kind of table. There was a medicinal smell in the air.

Sick bay. What am I doing in a sick bay?

The pilot and the monster were talking.

"Preed, you're in my light."

"Ah, such motherly concern for the subject!"

Cale took a better look at the pilot. She *was* beautiful. He felt another stirring.

And all of a sudden, he realized he was *naked*.

Uh-oh! Negative down there, negative, negative, no blood flow, okay?

It wasn't too hard to lose interest. All he had to do was look at the monster that wanted to *eat* him.

"Hey! Where are my clothes?"

They ignored him.

"Why, you positively glow with maternal warmth, Akima. It's very fetching." The monster paused. "I must have you."

"In your dreams, Preed, you pervert."

Korso. He'd met Korso at lunch. The man had gotten him off of Tau-14 in an Akrennian fighter—or what was left of it—which had cracked the canopy—

"Akrennians don't dream, remember?" the monster said.

"They don't *bathe* much either."

Korso had told him to exhale—and then. . . .

He was lucky to be alive. Fine. Now to more pressing matters. "Hey, I'm still *naked* down here!"

"Relax," it was the pilot, "we're just making sure you didn't get all broken."

She turned to the alien. "Give me the probe."

The probe?

Perhaps he'd been hasty in his estimate. Cale didn't feel very lucky at this particular instant. He felt even less fortunate as the pilot—the alien had called her Akima—was handed a huge, painful-looking device. It was large, with what looked like a motor on one end. The other end tapered to a fine point that looked remarkably like one of the devices from the holo he'd borrowed from Tynan. It seemed made to *insert*.

"You know, I'm feeling much better now."

Cale squirmed as Akima leaned forward with the probe in hand.

"This is great," Akima said. "Cross half the galaxy, nearly get our butts shot off by the Drej, just so we can rescue the window washer!"

For a second, Cale forgot the probe.

She remembers me!

And then he braced as she stuck it—in his ear. *Whew*.

"Hey, for your information, I happen to be Humanity's last great hope."

The Akrennian—Preed?—let out a laugh. "I weep for your species."

Akima checked a readout and then yanked the probe out of Cale's ear.

"Ow!"

"You're fine."

She did something with her foot, and then Cale felt himself tilting as the examination table tipped forward, standing him up.

He waved his hand a bit.

"I mean, I'm the guy with the *map* here. This is big medicine, right?"

Akima gave him a look.

"Big medicine. Sure. Let me see."

It seemed like he just couldn't get ahead. Get blasted into vacuum with*out* a suit, wake up naked in front of his fantasy girl and a monster, and no one seemed to *care*.

Akima leaned forward and took his hand in hers. Her hands were strong, but gentle. They felt good.

Some bit of hardness seemed to drop out of the pilot as she looked at the silvery tracings on Cale's hand.

"This is really it, then." She paused. "It can save us."

She stared at his palm even more intently, and traced a finger over some of the silvery whirls. The touch sent a tingle up Cale's back, and he felt a rushing *heat*.

"Uh, yeah, I guess . . ."

Her fingers felt good. And he was still *naked*.

"Do you know what this means?" she asked.

Cale didn't have any idea, except that if it meant she would keep holding his hand and running her fingers over it, it was all right with him.

"Uh, I'm really wanting those pants right about now . . ."

Akima looked at him, a slight smile on her face, and squeezed his hand.

But as with everything that had happened to him today, the good parts didn't last.

Came the monster. "Akima, my pet, might I remind you that if the boy isn't at death's door, Korso wants Gune to check the map so we can set a course. Do you *mind? Are we through pawing?* This is the *Valkyrie*, not a mating room."

Akima glared at Preed, which made Cale like her even more. "We're done," she said. She slapped the straplock release, and Cale quickly stepped away from the examination table and started looking for his clothes.

Cale turned around, trying to hide his embarrassment at the whole situation. Were they going to let him walk around naked all day? Cale hadn't ever had any modesty issues on Tau-14, but there had never been any girls like Akima at the communal showers there, either.

"You know, I never said I was going to help you guys. We never even addressed what's in it for me."

Preed smiled at Cale, revealing a *lot* of teeth. "Why, you get to be a *hero*."

Akima walked across the sick bay.

"Hero? Come on. I mean there must be something on the *Titan* worth selling, or trading or something. What, we're going to risk our necks to help out a bunch of drifter colony bums?"

Okay, guess I have to ask. "And where are my pants?"

Akima threw them at him—*smack*—they hit him right in the face.

Why'd she go and do a thing like that? There was some chemistry there, right?

The pilot stalked from the room, not looking back.

Preed grinned. "Want to guess where Akima grew up, Human?"

Uh-oh. "Uh—a drifter colony?"

Though it didn't seem possible, the alien's smile seemed to get larger. "The boy learns. Yes, the boy learns."

Cale followed Preed down one of the *Valkyrie*'s corridors. What a ship! It was gorgeous, everything he'd imagined looking at it from the outside. Tip-top shape and fairly humming with power.

He'd love to fly her.

Sure, with the impression you've made on Akima, that's real likely.

Well, maybe he'd just better cut some kind of deal with Korso and get out of here.

"Look, where's Korso? I want to talk to him."

Preed smiled his oily smile. "Why, I believe he's in navigation. In fact, here's a surprise, we're headed there now!"

Talking to Preed, Cale at first missed seeing the massive alien coming from the other direction along the corridor. Preed quickly ducked out of the way, but the new arrival stepped on Cale's foot with a foot that could only be called *enormous.*

"Hey, ow! You wanna watch who you're stepping on!"

The huge alien, crouched low in the walkway that had been designed for Humans, grabbed and shoved Cale up against the wall. He dangled like a child's doll in the alien's grip. He was terrified, but oddly enough, he noticed a pleasant smell about the big creature, it reminded Cale of the 'ponic flower gardens. What was that flower? Honeysuckle—?

"Watch it or you'll do *what*, Human?"

Cale looked at the angry birdlike beak of the alien and put it together with the huge feet.

A Mantrin.

Cale had heard a story once from another salvage guy about a Mantrin who had cleaned out a bar of Humans and aliens just because someone had told a joke about big feet. Apparently the joke hadn't even been directed at the Mantrin, who had just *happened* to hear it and the accompanying laughter and had taken offense.

Whatever kind of big medicine he had on his palm probably wouldn't impress this one.

Fortunately, Preed spoke up. "And behold, here is the lovely and talented Stith. This is Cale. You remember *Cale*?"

"No," said the big alien with a growl. "And I don't have time for *talk*. We lost targeting on one of our aft turrets again. What do you think this is, a *ferry*?" The alien released Cale, who slid to the deck.

"Get out of my—" At that moment, the case Stith carried somehow tipped open, spilling tools all over the corridor floor.

The big alien shouted something in a language Cale didn't recognize, but he'd bet a spaceship to a spoiled spud it was a curse of some kind. Stith squatted to pick up the tools.

Cale took a deep breath. The nice smell wasn't worth the ride. *Let's move along, shall we?* He hurried away from the mumbling Stith and caught up to Preed, who had already put some distance between himself and the alien.

"She's a sweet little thing, really. Weapons specialist. Normally, she's very good-natured."

Behind them Cale could hear the Mantrin. "*Great!* Things aren't bad enough! Damn *tools* all over the floor!"

"Fight the good fight, precious!" Preed called over his shoulder.

A bolt flew past Cale's head, just missing Preed.

"I'll kill you, Preed! How about I *kill* you!"

Preed and Cale hurried down the corridor. Cale took a deep breath, let it out.

Boy, they were having fun now.

—11—

C ale stood with Preed outside a metal door labeled "Navigation," and wondered what new twists this already twisted day would take.

Preed tapped on the door.

No answer.

Then after what seemed like a long time, from inside came a voice. "Must go to plan B. *Yes.* Must go to plan *B*." But whoever it was, they weren't talking to Preed and Cale.

Preed, who had so far impressed Cale only in his ugliness and the consistency of his oily manner, seemed to get a little exasperated. "*Gune!* Guney! Open the door."

There was still no answer, and after a few moments there was the sound of a crash. Not a particularly loud crash, more soft-thumpy than kitchen-pan.

Came the voice again. "Okay. I must multiply the mass by the acceleration, multiply by the coefficient of the friction, apply the necessary force—"

Preed looked at Cale and gave a little shrug. "Guess I'll have to use my universal key."

He did something with the lock and the door opened. "Gune?" he said.

Cale's eyes went wide as he stepped into the room. What a workshop! It was like stepping into a mad scientist's lab from an old fright-holo, only the tools were all *real*. If only he'd had access to this stuff when he was building *The Escape*! There was a Herumin matter recycler, a Moffat circuit printer—whoa, was that a Harsch ultrameter?

So busy was Cale looking at the equipment, he nearly missed the source of the voice he and Preed had heard from outside.

A short alien holding a ball-shaped object stepped toward Preed.

Whatever race Gune was, Cale had never seen one like him before. The little creature had huge eyes that reminded him of spotlights—focused and intense. A closer look revealed that Gune was wearing some kind of vision enhancement, which probably explained, at least *partially,* the giant size of the creature's pupils. His nose, or beak, or whatever, had a big stripe around the middle of it, a different color than the rest of the nose. Or beak. Or whatever.

"Does this look familiar?" Gune asked Preed. "Do you know what it is?"

Preed shook his head. "Never saw anything like it before."

"Neither have I! And yet I'm pretty sure I made it last night in my sleep! Apparently I used Gindrogac— highly unstable, Gindrogac is, you know."

Cale's gaze was caught by a three-dimensional model of this section of the galactic spiral. Something was *wrong* about it . . . Aha! The spin was off. Maybe he could *adjust* it a little. . . .

Behind him Cale heard Preed try to reach Gune again. "Gune?"

"I put a button on it. Yes, I wish to press it, but I'm not sure what it will *do*! One ought to know what a thing will do, oughtn't one, before pushing the button to make it do it?"

Cale had reached the controls for the map and began tapping corrections to the gyro subroutine that made it go.

This at last got Gune's attention.

"Ah, no! No, no, no, no! Careful please! Please! That is a work in progress! Progress, I say!"

Cale, now as immersed in his project as Gune had been, didn't pay any attention until—

Got it.

The model stabilized, the stars and systems now moving in harmony.

"There we go," he said. "Now it's right."

Gune had come alongside Cale now. "Oh, yes. Very good."

They laughed.

Cale indicated the display. "So, where are we now?"

Gune pointed to a section of systems at about the middle of the spinning map. "We are *here*. Right here. Bellasan Quadrant."

"About three million keks from Tau-14," added Preed. "Why—are you homesick?"

Cale was silent for a moment. "Gotta have a home for that," he said. "Not my problem." Maybe he missed Tek a little, but that was all. One place was as good as another.

Gune focused his huge eyes on Cale.

"Hmm. A Human. Translucent bipedal, mesomorphic, slightly postembryonic, and male, judging from the lack of mammary development. To be perfectly sure, I

will need you to remove your lower garments to check
for—"

"Yo, Gune." Preed managed to grab Gune's attention
before he went into another fit of concentration. He took
Cale's hand and waved it in front of the spotlight eyes.
"That's fascinating and all, the embryowhatsit, but take
a look at *this*. It's a map. Can you read it?"

The little alien seemed to stand up straighter for a
second. "I know it's a map! Can I read it? Of *course* I
can read it! Yes! Hmm! . . ."

Gune grabbed Cale's hand and yanked him closer,
looking at the silvery tracings.

The little navigator twisted Cale's hand left and right,
trying to line it up with the three-dimensional display.
He was strong for his size. The Human twisted left and
right as well, doing his best to keep his arm from breaking. Unfortunately, this meant a few crashes into the
equipment on nearby tables.

Hey!

Preed, apparently already familiar with Gune's meth-
ods, had wisely stepped back.

All at once, the little alien stopped.

"So what do you see?" asked Cale.

Gune pointed at a tiny speck of silver on Cale's palm.
"This is Pl'ochda. And this"—the finger stabbed a little
farther away—"this is Solbrecht! And this—and this . . .
what is *this?*"

Cale took a look. It looked like—ET meatballs? He
couldn't believe it.

*Either it stains more than the last batch Cook made,
or the sick bay autopreclean here really sucks.*

"Uh—that's lunch."

Gune seemed delighted with this information. "Oh,
it's *lunch!*" More quickly than Cale would have thought
possible, the little alien leaned down and licked the spot.

"Mmm. Spaghetti derivative. Meatballs—sort of, any-way—and . . . Caldroch droppings? Who ate it before you did?"

There was a thought Cale had never considered. Eeuuww!

Gune took another slurp.

"Hey, hey!"

Gune laughed.

Cale turned toward Preed. "Tell you a secret—this guy's nuts!"

Preed said, "No secret to me, pal."

From behind Cale came Korso's voice. "I'll tell you another."

Cale turned to look at the new arrival.

"He's never wrong. Got a mind like a mainframe. So where are we going, Gune?"

Gune took Cale's hand and held it toward Korso. "Ahhh . . . the broken moon of Sesharrim. About thir-teen thousand keks away."

"Have Akima lay in a course," Korso said to Preed, who immediately went out the door.

"Is that where the *Titan* is?" asked Cale.

"No, no, no." said Gune. "This is a broken moon." He indicated where on Cale's hand the moon was, and then followed an arc of silver up the palm.

"This is . . . mystery for thinking about . . . not clear yet, not yet."

"Well, it's a start," said Korso. He turned to Cale. "Come on, kid. I'll buy you a drink. We got things to talk about."

—12—

Akima stomped into the cockpit of the *Valkyrie*—at least as much as she *could* stomp, given that the decking was thick plasteel.

What an idiot!

He had no idea what kind of people lived on drifter colonies. No concept of how hard her grandmother had worked—*suffered*—to give her children a chance to do better.

I'd like to go back there and—

The pilot looked for a place to slam her fist—no, not the control panel, too easy to damage—there was a panel off from the auxiliary gun controls, something Stith had been tracing, had to be careful there—

Aha! Akima saw a spot that wasn't covered with instruments or near sensitive components.

The ceiling.

She slammed the side of her fist, hammer style, up toward the ceiling. Unfortunately, even though the ceiling was relatively low, the angle was such that the impact was less than satisfying. A kind of weak *tumf*.

Damn, damn, damn!

It wasn't the first time Akima had heard Humans who didn't live on drifter colonies badmouth those who did. It was a common enough attitude. Drifter colonists were "Losers living off alien charity" or "Happy they didn't have to do real jobs." And so many times, "Lazy bums who don't even *want* to work."

It was so *untrue*!

Houston, where she had grown up, had been lucky enough to snag work from alien companies. It wasn't *great* work, but she knew of many colonies that hadn't even gotten that much.

Most of the time Akima was able to shrug off the judgments she heard. But this time it hurt.

Why?

Her anger forgotten for a moment, Akima considered her question. When she'd been seven, she'd learned a valuable lesson from her grandmother. She and one of the other girls in the commune had been given a fake jewelry set as a treat. It had been full of outrageously large jewels that Akima had immediately made into treasure cargo for her cardbox spaceship. Her grandmother had made the children promise to share, but as with so many of the conditions little children agree to, Akima hadn't considered the real implications. She'd hit her friend Yukio when she had come to take her turn with the jewelry.

That had been a mistake.

When her grandmother had gotten home, the house had shook. Granny had grabbed little Akima and then, when the little girl had been sure blows were to come, her grandmother had asked, "Why?"

Akima hadn't been able to answer. Her grandmother had sat with her and explored the various paths her mind could have taken. Had Yukio tried to hit *her*? Didn't she remember the agreement to share? Or was it something else?

It had been a long and horrible process. Akima knew she hadn't wanted to share, *had* remembered the agreement, and when really pressed to think, had realized she'd done it because it would make her friend scared and run away.

It was nothing she'd consciously *thought* when she'd raised her hand, but it horrified her. Little Akima had cried and cried, and was so ashamed she'd given the jewels to Yukio to keep.

Her grandmother had smiled. "You have done well, little 'kima. You may avoid stupid ways of trying to reach a goal when you examine such ways *before* acting. Always *think,* my child."

She'd never met Cale before today. Why should his opinion about her origins matter?

Was it the map?

Here was someone who possibly had the key to finding the *Titan,* the lost super-ship from Humanity's darkest day. It might have enough range and power to take entire drifter colonies to a place where Humanity could rebuild.

And yet it seemed he would rather bargain to sell his birthright than assume it.

How stupid could he be? Did he have no compassion for the rest of his *species*? What kind of fool was he?

I'm starting to think like my grandmother.

Is that the real reason, eh, 'kima?

Akima squirmed on her chair a little as she considered another possibility. No. There was nothing else there. He was just a stupid salvage rat, a *boy.*

Is that why you got butterflies holding his hand?

No. There were no butterflies. What she'd felt holding his hand—it meant nothing. She did *not* feel hurt by

what he'd said because she wanted *him* to *like* her. No
way—

There was a chime from the door. Akima keyed the
commo.

"What do *you* want, Preed?"

"Well, my beautiful pilot, as I've already said, I want
you."

"Tough luck, Preed. If that's all, you can go howl at
the stars."

"Well, no, actually, Korso has a change of course.
Would you like to open the door, or shall I just go back
and let him know you aren't following his orders today?"

Akima cancelled the override she'd installed for
Preed's universal key. *He* certainly wouldn't be making
any surprise visits. Whatever she might—but probably
almost certainly—did *not* feel about Cale, her thoughts
about Preed were crystal clear.

No way.

Involuntarily the memory of touching Cale's hand
popped into her head.

I wonder what he's up to.

Cale stood next to Korso and watched the homemade
drink distiller slowly spit out another drop of green goo.
At the rate the machine was going, Korso and Cale
wouldn't be drinking until sometime in the next week.

Gee, yeah, I can't wait to have a drink of that.

Cale didn't say anything though, because Korso did
not look happy that his machine wasn't performing for
company.

The older man shrugged. "She's a little bit—twitchy.
Hold on. There's a little technical adjustment that sometimes works—"

Korso kicked the hell out of the machine.

Cale grinned. He'd used that adjustment method himself—but only after reasonable efforts failed.

Korso's "adjustment" knocked several glops into the now half-full glass of green syrup.

"That didn't help much, did it?" Cale said. "Let me have a look at it."

Korso stood back after kicking the machine one last time. Punishing it, Cale figured. There was definitely a different attitude to that last kick.

The machine was fairly simple; it just looked like a few of the distilling tubes had gummed up. Cale began adjusting the backflow valve to clear them.

"So what's on this broken moon, anyway?"

"A race called the Gaoul. They're pretty much the only intelligent life there. At least that's what I've heard."

"They're just going to lead us right to the *Titan*?"

"Well, now. Do I finally detect *interest* in your voice in finding the *Titan*?"

Cale looked up from the valves. "Hey, back off. The *Titan*'s my ticket, that's all. I figure anything people are trying to kill me for has got to be worth a lot of cash."

"So now you're gonna play tough, huh? Gotta be worth something because they want to kill *you*?"

Cale spun the backflow valve to "off" and turned around. He glared at Korso. "Do I look like I'm playing to *you*?"

Korso glared right back. "You *look* like your father."

Cale did his best not to show it, but the comment threw him. There was the instant anger he felt whenever he thought of his father—who had *abandoned* him when he'd been a boy. And yet, there was a certain pleasure in being compared to his dad—

He was like me?

No. He was *not*.

I would never, ever abandon someone.

A tension built between the two men, stretched—

And broke, as there was the sound of a soft clunk from behind Cale. The drink machine had started working again. Cale turned to see, and watched as a thick, green liquid poured into the cup, steam rising from it. When the cup had filled, Korso picked it up and took a sip.

A second cup followed the first. Cale took it and lifted it suspiciously to his nose, sniffing before taking a sip. There was a pleasant tangy odor, which reminded him of something Tek had once showed him. It had been a yellow fruit that the old alien had secretly grown in the hydroponic gardens. A lemon he'd called it.

Cale sipped the drink. It was pretty good. Maybe Korso wasn't such a bad guy after all.

"Your father was good with machines, too."

No, Cale thought, *strike that*. He was all bad. Couldn't he think of something else to talk about? Some *one*? Cale tried to push the subject away.

"Yeah, well, I don't remember."

But Korso would not be swayed. "He built the *Titan*. Most advanced ship in the galaxy. Fully self-sustaining energy system—the science was way above me, I couldn't begin to explain it. But he believed it was the key to finding a new home world. He said in time—"

Cale had had enough. "In time? In *time*? It's been fifteen years. How long did he want us to wait? If he knew where another world for the human race was, why not just *tell* us?"

"This wasn't plan A, kid. He knew the Drej would come after him. That's why he left the map with you and left you—so they'd look for him and not you."

Korso paused, and he and Cale moved to a small table near a kleersteel portal. The stars rushed by outside, their colors Dopplering as the ship shot through space.

It was beautiful. Cale wished he could enjoy it without the accompanying conversation. But no—

"And they found him. But before he died, he hid the *Titan*. The only way to find it is on your hand."

There it was. Gold engraved and on a platter. Cale couldn't believe Korso would give him such an easy win. But he'd take it.

Want to ram my father down my throat, eh?

"So you're really counting on me, then."

"Everyone is."

Cale let out a cool smile. "Well, I'll tell you. If I don't like the way things are going, I'll show you just how much like my father I really am."

Korso looked confused; he hadn't expected this.

"So watch your mouth, friend. I'm the guy you need, and if you throw too much crap at me, I will hop off at the nearest rock, and you can go whistle for my map, you copy?"

There. That felt a lot better.

— 13 —

C ale waited on the hoversled with Akima, Korso, and Stith. The hydraulics whined a bit and the door to the cargo bay of the *Valkyrie* began to open. There was a slight hiss as the overpressurized air from the cargo bay matched pressure with the atmosphere.

Cale let out the breath he'd been holding as Akima raised the sled and took them out.

Relax, there is air *here, you don't need a pressure suit, it's* safe.

Years of living on Tau-14 had left him surprisingly unprepared to go outside on an oxy-world. He glanced around. No one seemed to have noticed. Then he took a look and realized why. Everyone was looking at the scenery.

The world of Sesharrim was extraordinary. The *Valkyrie* sat on the edge of a large coral reef, which was a bright red. The ocean which surrounded her was also red—actually more of a deep maroon, but stunning. Over all of this hung the moon—called the broken moon for a good reason. It looked like some giant creature had taken a bite out of it and in the process split it into two halves. The odd mass added a kind of eerie quality to the scene.

A few miles distant was a shoreline. Cale squinted a bit, trying to get a closer look. He knew from their over-flight that there were some ruins there, but couldn't see them from this angle. He could make out the coral arch that he'd seen on the way in. It was *huge*.

There were a few of those odd trees visible there. Something about them—

Korso turned to Preed and Gune, who stood on the edge of the reef. "We'll take the sled and see if we can find the Gauol. Preed, you and Gune watch the ship."

"Watch the ship?" Gune said. The little alien looked profoundly disappointed and stared longingly at the dis-tant landmass. "Watch it do what? It will be the same later as now."

"Just stay here. You are too valuable to risk."

Preed looked relieved.

"And keep the engines hot," added Korso.

Preed grinned revealing his huge incisors. "Oh, yes, they'll be nice and toasty. I'm *not* keen to have the Drej catch us with our shirts down."

"That's 'pants' down," Korso said.

"Whatever."

Korso gave a wave, then nodded to Akima, then they were off.

As they approached the shore, Cale understood what had seemed odd about the trees in the distance.

They were *floating*. What the *hell*?

Thin roots—or maybe they should be called tethers—held the trees to the ground. What had looked like leaves seemed to be some kind of baglike shapes. Some of the trees were closer to the ground than others, and Akima chose a high tree to go under for their exit from the ocean.

Korso reached over and put his arm on Cale's shoulders. "Welcome to the planet Sesharrim."

Cale twisted away from Korso's arm.

First he says I look like my father, then he tries to act like him. What is this guy's angle?

Cale was abruptly aware of an odor. No, it was rank. Dead fish? Rotted ET meatballs? Euuuugh. What *was* it?

He looked over at Korso. "The place *stinks*, Captain. Thanks *so* much for bringing me here."

Korso glared for a second. "The *smell* is leakage from the hydrogen trees." He indicated the huge trees hovering over the sled. "Mixes with the local air and makes a kind of sulfur compound."

"Yeah, right. Fascinating."

"Good thing Akima here is such a good pilot—if we clip one of those, we'll be blown to bits. Hydrogen and air together can be volatile, you know."

"I was a junk jockey, I know about gases, thank you." But Cale eyed the trees with a bit more respect.

A few minutes later they came to the outskirts of the ruins. Whatever society had lived here before seemed to have built their structures along a modified version of Greek architecture. Huge columns supported massive pediments, and all around were blocks of red stone.

There was no sign that anyone had lived here for a long time. The buildings all seemed long deserted, and most of them had more than one wall knocked down.

Cale noticed that it was getting darker. The broken moon was now shining more visibly than it had before.

This is creepy.

He snuck a peek at Akima. She didn't seem angry

anymore, but he wanted to take it carefully. Had to figure out a way to get around the screwup his mouth had gotten him into.

She looked *good*. Strong, too, as she piloted the hoversled.

I'd like to see her fly the Valkyrie.

Sure. He'd like to see her do a *lot* of things, but that was all unlikely at the moment.

The sled reached what looked like a central square of some kind, and Akima throttled back. The group climbed down from the sled and walked toward the middle of the square.

"Hello!" called Korso, "Is there anybody here? We're looking for the Gauol!"

There was no answer. In the distance was the sound of some wind blowing over *something*. *Really* creepy.

Cale had an idea for starting a conversation with Akima.

"What exactly do the Gauol look like?" he asked directing the question to her.

Akima just shrugged.

Well, that was excellent. Way to go, Cale. A shrug. Keep going, you might get a sneer.

"We don't know," said Korso, filling the silence. "They don't get out much."

In the distance, off to Korso's right, Cale saw a flash. *What?*

There, just at the outside of his peripheral vision, there it was again.

Cale glanced over at Stith. The big alien looked back at him and nodded. Yep, she'd seen it too.

A second or two later there was another flash—only this time it stayed lit. A narrow slit of light was sitting on *top* of a column. A column between where they were and the hoversled.

"We have a kid here with a map you guys should know about!" Korso yelled.

If he calls me kid *one more time. . . .*

But then Cale forgot about that, for there was a loud, rushing sound that was definitely getting closer.

Keep calm here, keep calm!

They were a tough group. Hell, he and Korso had faced down Drej. This was a *dead* city. No reason to be nervous, it was just, uh, the *wind*. They had big winds on planets, right?

Cale took another look at Stith. The female Mantrin's eyes were busy, scanning all around. Her fingers played over her rifle-sized photon weapon. She looked nervous.

Uh-oh.

Anything that made *Stith* that nervous. . . .

And suddenly he saw them: A huge cloud of flying things, spiraling down from the giant coral arch that was far overhead. They seemed small at first, but then Cale realized they were larger than he had thought. *Much* larger. They were tall and thin, red like the oceans and the coral, and had sharp looking triangular heads. The creatures had double sets of wings that reminded Cale of his Earth studies with Tek. Creatures that had lived on Terra—

Bats *they were called.*

But the bats Cale had studied pictures of on Tek's computer were *not* this big. And there had been no mention of white, glowing eyes.

The cloud of aliens reached them. They landed all around, on every spot available, clustered so thick they seemed almost solid, until the team was completely surrounded.

Cale stared at the frightening aliens enclosing them.

All at once the creatures began screaming. The sound did *not* indicate goodwill, in Cale's opinion.

"I guess we know what happened to the Gauol," Cale said. "Man!"

Cale stared at Korso. The image the older man had painted was particularly grim. He could imagine the villagers walking along, happily, until out of the sky came these blood-red nightmares to *eat* them all—

I wish I'd stayed with the ship.

"Give me an option here, Stith."

Stith took a long look around. "Blast 'em?" she suggested.

"All of them? That's creative. Thanks a lot."

"I'm in," said Cale. "Shoot now, and don't ask questions later."

The creatures stared intently at the party.

Korso nodded, his nervousness apparent. "Okay. Open fire, on five. We'll clear a path to the sled."

"Hold on," Akima said. "Think about it for a second."

"Think about what?" Cale said. "Being eaten?"

Cale estimated the distance between them and the sled. It did not look good. If these creatures had wiped out the Gauol. . . .

"One . . . two . . . three—"

"Wait! Wait! Look what they're doing!" Akima pointed at a group of creatures that seemed to be focused on Cale.

Yeah, they're getting ready to eat *me. Thanks for the update.*

Well, at least she cared enough about him enough to notice.

Korso shook his head at her. "If these things killed the Gauol, what makes you think that—?"

"I think these things *are* the Gauol."

Hello? Why hadn't he thought of that? Cale took a deep breath. If she were right, they might make it out of here. Only one way to find out though—

He held his hand out toward the possibly-Gaoul.

There was a rustling as the creatures shifted, taking a closer look, but no threatening moves.

A larger alien moved out from the surrounding group, he looked like the others, except with *horns* on his head.

Korso motioned to Stith to keep cool. She nodded, but kept her weapon held ready.

The large alien made a huge sweeping motion with a wing and pointed it toward the sky.

The moon. It was pointing at the moon.

"Ah, yeah, the moon. That's how we knew to come here." Cale extended his hand toward the nightmarish alien. "My father made a map with that moon in it. Wait—is the ship hidden there?"

The alien abruptly grabbed Cale by the shoulders and turned him to face the moon. It raised its wing again, covering the moon with the tip of it. Again it did this, and looked at Cale.

It wants me to raise my wing? Oh—

Cale lifted his map-hand up to cover the moon. He held his palm open, and saw that four stars were now lined up, one each in the V between each finger. The silvery symbols on his hand were clearly pointing toward a distant clustering of stars. It was a perfect fit. Only by standing here on this world could it have worked.

Wow. That means. . . .

Akima bent close to him, and he took a breath, catching the spicy scent she was wearing. She put her head alongside his and looked up at his hand.

It seemed pretty romantic for a second, until Korso joined her on the other side.

"It's somewhere in the Andali Nebula," said Akima.

"I'll be damned," Korso said. "We did it, kid! The *Titan* is as good as ours."

Cale was too busy thinking to worry about the "kid."

"He must have been here. Standing *right* here, on this world . . ."

Akima heard him. "Who?"

"My father," whispered Cale.

Suddenly there was a deep rumbling.

Cale looked up in time to see several midnight blue ships roar past. They blotted out his view of the nebula.

Oh, *shit.*

Look who was coming to visit!

—14—

Cale froze. Drej, *here? How'd they get here? Oh-shit-oh-shit-oh-*shit*!*

"GO!" Korso bellowed.

Go? Go where? We're screwed.

"Get to the *beach*! We'll call the *Valkyrie*!"

Yeah, right. Might as well call for an ice-cream smashee while we're at it.

But Cale followed Korso. Akima was on his left, and behind him he could hear Stith's big pounding footsteps. The sled, unfortunately, was at the edge of the big courtyard. Even more unfortunate was the pulse of laser light that flared and stabbed past Cale.

Gauol flew left and right, taking off to get out of the way.

If I had wings I'd be flying, too.

Cale risked a look over his shoulder and saw a trio of Drej stinger ships diving toward the courtyard.

How did they *find* us*?*

They weren't going to make it. It was too far to the sled, and the ships were closing, Cale could just *feel* it.

All at once, a group of the Gauol dove right at them. Cale felt tiny, bony hands grabbing him on each arm, and suddenly he *was* flying. Not alone, either. The rest of the group had been airlifted as well.

They were taken straight up into a hydrogen tree. It was a good tactical move—apparently the Drej had read up on the trees because they held their fire.

The implications weren't lost on Cale.

They want me alive.

Their flying friends were *good*. No, better than that. Cale had never seen such aerobatics. Being born with wings made a difference.

The stingers were quickly lost amid the tiny vines and huge hydrogen filled bladders of the trees. The smell was bad, sure, but Cale figured it was better than the alternative.

He heard a roaring sound and saw the three stingers peel off toward the *Valkyrie*.

I hope Gune and Preed are okay.

The Gauol managed to get their cargo to the hoversled.

When, of course, *more* stingers came arcing down from the sky.

Stith unlimbered the huge weapon she'd been carrying, thumbed a few switches, and fired.

A bright blast of light filled the night and two of the ships exploded, sending a third spinning off into the night. Two with one shot. Outstanding!

"Come to Stith, vermin! Come to me! Hahha!"

Akima fired up the thrusters and spun the sled around while Cale dove for the mooring line.

Korso was on his commo. "Preed, come in! Preed, where are you?!"

Akima shouted at Cale, pointing at a cable loop on the side of the sled. "Hang on!"

The sled blasted off.

The ride out was much bumpier than the ride in.

They skimmed the edges of the hydrogen trees, comfort sacrificed for speed as Akima pushed the sled's impellers to the limit. A group of Gauol flew cover, attempting to mask the sled with their bodies.

Unfortunately, it not only wasn't working, but it was hampering the shooting angles for the defenders on the sled. Across from where he clung, Cale saw a stinger shift in formation to take advantage of the fact that his side of the sled wasn't as well defended as Stith's. As he watched the stinger draw closer, Cale could hear Preed on the commo.

"Captain, we're on our way. We can't *see* you, though—where are you?"

"We're in the hydrogen trees! See if you can spot the Drej and you'll find *us*. And burn the fuel, Preed!"

Cale realized that Stith didn't see the new threat. He looked around. It was up to him.

The bumpy ride didn't make for a great shooting platform, but the stinger was getting *closer* and he had to try *now*.

Cale fired, and surprising himself, hit the stinger's port engine, sending it pinwheeling off into a fireball.

Unfortunately, the huge slug-thrower Korso had given him carried quite a mean kick. That, coupled with the fact that the sled chose that moment to take a quick dip, sent him flying over the edge. He grabbed for the cable loop and got it.

Somehow Akima saw. "Hang on, Cale!"

The cable was slippery. Very slippery. Cale tried to hook his wrist in it, but the angle was all wrong. Then he had the same kind of sick realization he'd had the day he nearly missed the docking tower on Tau-14.

I'm not going to make it.

"Whoaa!"

He lost his grip and started to fall—just in time to feel a hand grab his ankle. It was Akima!

Akima? Who's flying this thing?

"Cale!"

The physics of the situation, however, hadn't improved. Akima must have dived to reach him, because she was leaning *way* over the edge of the sled.

"Ahh!"

They fell together into the red ocean.

The fluid was a lot warmer than Cale would have expected. They came up sputtering, and fortunately, the liquid was dense enough so they could float in it. Must be mostly water.

Wonder if anything hungry lived in it?

The sled kept going.

He and Akima treaded water and watched as the hoversled shot off into the distance. Cale couldn't believe it. Half of the group falls overboard, but no one notices?

Predictably, the Drej had. Laser bolts sizzled into the water nearby, and Cale fired his slug-thrower, which he had somehow kept hold of, hitting the ship.

Yes!

The ship wasn't badly damaged, however, and Cale cursed at it as it circled away.

Another stinger dove at them. Cale's gun suddenly went—*click!*—

Click? Uh-oh—

Dive! Dive! Dive! Down he went, pulling Akima with him.

The red water refracted the laser beams away from them. But they had to come up . . . for . . . *air!*

A green cone of light enveloped them as they resurfaced. This was good and bad: Good, in that it wasn't a killing laser. Bad, in that it turned out to be a tractor beam, and the next thing Cale knew, he and Akima were floating high over the red ocean. Several of the stinger ships had joined together into one vessel above them. Cale watched the process and couldn't help but wonder how they did it.

Then he saw a door of some kind open on the bottom of the newly formed ship. The green beam carried them straight toward it. Cale looked at Akima.

Any ideas?

She shook her head.

They were in trouble all right.

Cale watched Akima lean over and peer out a clear porthole in their cell. He'd already seen what was outside: nothing. They were in space, somewhere, trapped, caught, and truly in deep feces. And this was a very strange vessel, in so many ways he couldn't begin to unscramble them all. Very, very strange.

But, hey, Akima sure looked good. Cale watched the play of muscle in her legs as she leaned forward.

Okay, so we're doomed, but maybe we could enjoy our last moments together . . . ?"

Uh-huh. Cale figured that somehow that approach wouldn't work too well.

Akima broke the silence. "They're going to use you to figure out where the *Titan* is. Probably blow it up, too, when they find it."

The *Titan*? Who cared? He could think of a lot more important things to worry about at the moment.

"We have to find a way out of here, or we're *dead*," he said.

"No argument there," she said. "Maybe Korso will get to it first."

Again with the Titan*?*

"Why do you care so much about that thing?" he asked.

Cale was genuinely curious. The *Titan* was a ticket off Tau-14 for him, and maybe more, but at the moment he wasn't too happy with where it had taken him.

Like Tek had always said, no free lunch.

Akima moved a little closer to Cale and looked directly at him.

"I was raised around people—around Humans. Drifter colony bums, I believe, you called them."

Ouch.

"I barely remember Earth, but the older ones used to tell us about it so that the memory wouldn't be completely lost. Things got pretty hard on the colony, but those memories kept us going."

Akima's eyes had lost focus and she was staring off into the distance. Looking at her face, Cale thought that it was one of the most beautiful things he'd ever seen.

"We had a home once, Cale. The *Titan* is our chance to find one again."

She really believed it. Cale could see that.

"So I guess that's how I wound up here." Akima smiled and indicated the cell.

Cale smiled, too. At that moment he would have been happy to bring her the *Titan* giftwrapped, if only to keep seeing her smile.

Not likely with the Drej holding them.

The Drej. Cale felt a flash of fear that quickly changed to anger. All his life he'd had to suffer as a second-class citizen, and he had suffered personally at their hands, too. If those appendages could be called hands. This wasn't his first brush with the dreaded aliens, though it certainly was the most serious.

All the times he'd had to be last in line, or had hidden

from aliens like Po and Firrikash—it was the Drej's fault.

"Why didn't they just kill all of us? Why didn't they wipe out the Human race?" The words seemed to bubble out of their own accord.

Akima considered her answer. "Without a planet, without a base of operations, we were no longer considered dangerous. They are hive beings, they get their strength from proximity. With Humans scattered all over, they don't think of us as threatening. At least, that's the theory I heard. Nobody knows for sure how the Drej think."

Yeah, well, they've certainly gone a long way for a couple of nonthreatening Humans today.

It occurred to Cale that if the Drej thought his map was so important that they sent stinger ships all across the galaxy to chase him, maybe they were *scared* of what the *Titan* represented.

Could the *Titan* be used to *hurt* the Drej? There was no way to know.

But if it could . . . and if he could *get* to it . . . ?

He could use it to hurt *them.*

Yes. There was a nice thought. But first, he had to escape—which might not exactly be the easiest trick to pull off.

"So, I guess we'll just have to get away and kick their asses," he said.

She grinned at him, and he liked that—a lot.

"You're crazy, you know."

"Yeah. Well, it's something to do, isn't it?"

—15—

After what seemed like hours, their ship reached its destination.

Akima took periodic looks through the porthole. Cale couldn't figure out what she expected to spot, so he wasn't really paying attention when she let out a gasp.

"Cale! You have to *see* this."

Cale sat up and moved to the porthole. Ahead he saw the edges of *something*. Something *huge*. Giant black spires made up the outline of the shape that their ship was heading toward. Nearer their vessel, Cale could see something moving—it was the V-shape of a joined stinger ship. Size-wise, compared to the shape they were moving toward, the stinger looked like the head of a pencil next to a trash bin.

Oh, man!

A ship that size had to be six or seven keks tall. That made it twice the size of the *Titan*. Which meant . . .

"It's got to be—"

"The Drej mothership," finished Akima.

The Drej mothership was not a common sight to civ-

ilized worlds in this section of space—unless they were
about to be vaporized or their territory added to the Drej
hive. Cale had heard stories about it—unbelievable tales:
The ship never needed to refuel, it had the power to
create living Drej from inside it, there was a dimensional
gate inside that let the Drej come into this universe from
another—and more.

The tales couldn't all be true, or could they?

Well, maybe I'll just ask 'em.

Sure.

There was no feeling of slowing. Cale didn't really
think much about it until Akima brought it up.

"Uh, you might want to brace yourself, Cale."

"What?"

"By my calculations, we're going way too fast to de-
celerate to anything resembling docking speed before we
smash into the ship."

Cale took a turn at the porthole.

Shit, she's right.

Ahead of them was a black, featureless wall. Cale slid
to the side and Akima joined him near the viewport.
Their heads were almost touching as they watched the
black wall coming up fast.

They were almost on it.

Without thinking, Cale reached over and took Akima's hand. He squeezed it and she squeezed back as
their ship moved closer and close—

—and *through.*

What the hell?

The wall had done *something* as they impacted. It had
been too fast for Cale to be sure, but it had *looked* as if
they'd just . . . melted into it.

There had been a sudden slowdown after that, but
nothing like the impact that they had expected. It had
been like the ships had *flowed* together.

Cale turn to look out the porthole, only—the porthole was *gone*!

The cell they were in had changed.

Cale looked at Akima and she was as surprised as he was. At about that point he realized they were still holding hands. Akima must have realized it, too, because she started to say something—

The hatch opened.

There had been no hatch on that side of the cell before, so here was another surprise. Four Drej entered the cell. Two of them grabbed Akima, and two went for Cale.

Suddenly Akima lunged forward, tugged hard against the Drej. She managed to free an arm enough to put it around him, and he felt *something* being put into his pocket.

Huh?

The Drej quickly grabbed her again, and took her from the cell. Cale was marched out behind her, and realized they were being split apart only after he had exited.

Akima was nowhere in sight.

He was alone, a prisoner on the Drej mothership.

The ship was spookily silent.

The Drej certainly didn't seem to talk much. In fact, they didn't talk at all. They marched Cale along several long hallways. Eerie lighting and even stranger-looking Drej were everywhere. There were big ones, tall ones, small ones, and ones that seemed to have tools for arms. Their bodies glowed from the inside. Cale could see what looked like veins on some of them pulsing with what looked like *flows* of light.

Man!

There was no conversation, although Cale could see Drej moving nearer one another from time to time.

There would be pulses of light from one, and then more pulses from another.

Speaking with light?

The Drej escorting him didn't seem to be watching him too closely, so he took the time to examine the thing Akima had left in his pocket. First he used his fingers to try and map out what it could be. There seemed to be an Activation button and a Variable Adjusting knob. Possibly it was an audio sender of some kind.

As they went into a particularly dark area, Cale slipped the item from his pocket and palmed it. When the light improved, he took a look at it.

A translator!

Many pilots kept an electronic translator as part of their flight kit. If they ever wound up stranded where they didn't know the language, it could help them out of a tight spot.

But would it work on Drej? Was it set up to intercept light signals? Some societies used light, but could this thing understand that kind of communication? Some of the translators were configured to read photonic languages, but was this one?

Only one way to find out.

Cale eased the translator up to his collar and tucked it inside, leaving what he figured was a sensor of some kind exposed. His motions were casual, and he was very careful. The guards didn't notice a thing. Or at least they didn't *act* as if they did.

Thoughts played through his head as he clipped the translator on. Why hadn't Akima mentioned it before?

Maybe she thought someone might be listening.

Why had she given it to him? The only reason Cale could think of was that she wanted him to have an edge to escape if the chance came up. That she would do that for him made him feel both pleased and worried at the same time. He'd have given *her* an edge of course. . . .

He toggled the Activation switch and suddenly the ship was no longer silent.

"—adjust the *leihah* shielding to prepare for future leakage. Karaba—!"

"—Task leader? Yes, I have sent for more *enjah* for the *douheh*."

The conversation had to be coming from the Drej over by the wall there. They seemed to be doing some kind of maintenance work. All around him, Cale could suddenly understand the flashes of light he'd been seeing.

His guards were, unfortunately, silent. Cale could think of no way to engage them in conversation without giving away his edge. Besides, he didn't speak light. Could they hear spoken speech? And would they understand it if they could hear it? And if they did, would they care?

Just what he needed, more questions.

Ahead loomed a huge doorway. His captors slowed their pace and made some kind of gesture. The door opened.

The room was unlike anything he'd ever seen before. Giant honeycombed chambers surrounded a large open space. The architecture was *definitely* alien, more so than *anything* he had ever experienced.

The walls seemed to pulse with an internal glow, similar to the light coming from the Drej themselves. The whole place was so strange it seemed to almost be a dream of some kind. How could this be happening?

Maybe I'll wake up.

In the middle of the room was a raised structure. Large pieces of an odd biomechanical nature surrounded it and seemed to be somehow aimed at the structure.

His captors marched him over there.

Great.

Behind the structure were hundreds and hundreds of Drej soldiers standing absolutely still, only the pulsing of light in their bodies giving away the fact that they lived.

Talk about overkill. Two are doing just fine.

As he was marched onto the platform, Cale saw Akima, held against a wall by some unseen force. She was struggling, but unable to break whatever it was that held her. She saw Cale.

"Cale!" she called.

"Akima!"

Two other Drej soldiers joined the ones holding Cale. One took his hand, and the other made some adjustments to some kind of control panel. Some of the ominous instruments surrounding him seemed to move in a bit closer.

And then several beams of light suddenly switched on. They were sharply delineated, and all of them came together to focus on his palm.

Other than a little warmth, Cale didn't feel a thing.

What are they doing—?

And then he realized.

The map! They're reading the map!

"No!"

Cale tried to jerk his hand away from the Drej holding it. The alien was solid and strong, and all he was able to do was to wiggle a bit. A very little bit.

After what seemed like minutes, but was probably only a few seconds, the beams blinked off. There were muted sounds from the direction of the Drej by the panel.

The translator whispered to him, "—antenna array resolution successful. Holographic extrapolation seems to be in this sector—"

Suddenly a gigantic sphere appeared over Cale's head.

He wasn't the only surprised being in the chamber, though. Drej heads swiveled in surprise and then the assembled creatures somehow bowed.

The translator let him hear what the horrible looking face in the sphere was saying. Unlike the Drej that it had translated before, however, the voice from this being was not given much of a gender identity. It was neither male nor female, unlike anything he had ever heard. Were words simply tools in this being's mouth?

"We have our destination. Set a course for the Andali Nebula."

Oh, no!

The head in the sphere continued. "Keep the boy on board, he may yet be useful. Discard the girl."

Discard the—?

"No! Stop! Leave her alone—"

But it was too late. Cale watched, horrified, as the wall behind Akima suddenly seemed to melt around her, and she was sucked through. Gone.

Things were suddenly very real. Cale stared at the wall where Akima had been in complete shock.

They killed *her.*

So far it had been almost like playing Drej-and-Humans—like he had with a few of his friends as a boy. Bang! Shoot the bad guys, and the good guys get away.

All of a sudden, it wasn't a game.

The two Drej guards who had taken him from the cell grabbed his arms again and started to lead him away. Cale stared at the floor as they led him out of the chamber. Any doubts he'd had about where his loyalties lay were stilled. The Drej were utterly, truly, alien, and he was *Human.*

But what could he do about it?

Right at the moment, not a damned thing.

—16—

S he wasn't dead.
   Well, here's a surprise.
   Akima stared out at the blackness of space from
within the bluish cocoon that the Drej had encased her
in before ejecting her from the mothership. At the moment, the cocoon was all that was protecting her from
the vacuum of space.
   For now.
   There was no antigrav, no heat, and no discernable
oxy source in the cocoon. The Drej mothership seemed
to be rotating around her, but she knew that it was *her*
frame of reference that was wrong.
   The trip from the audience chamber, where she'd seen
Cale, had been interesting. The walls had dissolved, like
some kind of force field being turned off, and she'd shot
through them for what seemed like several minutes before winding up here. There had been an ozonelike smell
that had oddly comforted her as she was ejected from
the ship: It reminded her of hot electronics.
   For all she knew, the Drej hadn't planned to encase

her in the life-sustaining cocoon, but that it might be a by-product of traveling through their walls.

I wonder if they sent Cale out this way?

There were no other cocoons in sight.

The mothership seemed to be quickening its pace. It arced across her vision, seeming to come up from below.

Hmm, I seem to be spinning forward.

She didn't know what good the knowledge would do her, but she couldn't help working out her flight path. Akima did her best to figure out the course that the Drej were heading. If she managed to get away, the knowledge might help her find Cale again.

Cale.

She hoped he was all right. He'd been through a lot, but seemed to be learning who he was. The pilot wished she hadn't been separated from him. She remembered holding his hand in their cell. . . .

Okay, so maybe I do like him. A little.

They had been doing something to him. From the way he'd yelled, she figured it had to do with the map. Could their technology place the map in its proper context?

On her next turn around, Akima managed to get a fix on a distant star. If she was right, and that was Valaki, then somehow the Drej *had* read the map.

Another revolution confirmed it. The mothership was heading toward the Andali Nebula.

Shit.

The ship was getting more distant.

Come on, Korso, now would be a good time to come blasting up.

The air in the cocoon was running out. Akima could almost smell the extra carbon dioxide. Many years of training in space suits had taught her to sense when the scrubbers stopped working, or the air was about to run out. She figured she might have another half hour.

Not a good way to go, either.

Maybe she would fall asleep. It wasn't like she could light a signal fire or anything. Her arms were pinned to her sides. The feeling of helplessness made her breathe faster.

No, no! Got to breathe less. *Hold on as long as possible.*

The Drej ship was out of sight now.

A few more minutes passed. Akima spent the time thinking about her life. It had been pretty good. She'd almost brought the *Titan* home. Think of how her grandmother would have loved that! And she'd been able to do what she loved best—fly. She hoped her grandmother wouldn't be too upset.

She'd be out flying in the stars. Kind of like that dot over there—

A ship!

The ship came closer, a vector that was following the path of the Drej mothership. Could it be the *Valkyrie*?

Akima squinted, but couldn't tell. The ship moved closer.

She passed out.

Akima woke up to bad news.

First was the smell. It smelled like a toilet—a strong, uric acid smell.

Eugh.

Well, at least she was alive. Maybe she could just go back to sleep. Maybe this was a bad dream.

A hairy hand reached down and grabbed her face.

The being who had grabbed her was nonhuman, and plainly from a world that was cold. Hair covered his entire body,

"Waakke upp, Huuumaan!"

A frighteningly large grin split his head. Large fangs

gleamed in the low light of the room. Where was she?

Akima slapped his hand away.

"Ooooooh, so you're feeling better he? Too good to give old Krenie a kiss?"

Akima stood up and wobbled slightly. "I'll kiss you with these," she said, taking a guard stance. She was surprised with how weak her voice sounded.

"Guess you're okay, then," piped the hairy alien. He—she—it?—waved at something behind her. "Go ahead and let me out, Guadda."

Akima turned and saw—a Gvort.

Oh, shit.

Gvorts were slimy, squat aliens who cared little for most other species. This favor was returned by most, since the Gvort were slavers who would sell their best friends for a profit. There was a saying, "Never turn your back on a Gvort. When you turn around, you'll be in chains."

Akima looked at the alien, who regarded her just as closely.

"What is your name, Human?"

"What the hell do you care? I'm a bonded pilot with the flyer's guild. You can't hold me."

"Well, there we disagree," said the Gvort. The hairy alien had called it Guadda, Akima remembered.

"You know the rules, I found you, near death, and salvaged you. That makes you mine." The little toadlike alien stuck its tongue out and touched its nose with the tip.

"But don't worry, Human," and the Gvort smiled, revealing a red-gummed mouth with tiny teeth. "It's not for long."

Akima stared at the walls of her new cell. They were old plasticrete, pitted in places, and covered with tidbits

of graffiti. Some of the bits of wit were funny, some
more somber.

"Sometimes the wolves are silent and the moon
howls," one line went.

Wolves were an old Earth beast, she knew. Apparently Humans had been in this holding cell before.
Great.

The graffiti was underscored by a particularly large
line at the bottom of the wall: DON'T LET THEM SELL
YOU TO NARNO.

The words sent a chill up Akima's spine. *Sold.* She
was going to be *sold.*

Slavery wasn't approved of by most alien races, but
it was tolerated. In some sectors it was quasi-legal, in
the form of long-term contracts; in others, limited legal
status was granted to beings who were not citizens or
who had been 'salvaged' by unscrupulous beings. And
on some worlds, it was accepted practice. The pilot's
guild had a standing bond to all slavers to return any
pilots found floating in space, but apparently the Gvort
who had found her thought he could turn a better profit
this way. The planet she was on was apparently one of
the planets that operated with an open slave system.

The past day had seen her fall from pilot of a starship,
to prisoner of the Drej mothership, and then all the way
down to about-to-be-sold slave.

It was almost funny.

Well, at least it can't get much worse.

But then, of course, it did. The hallway outside the
cells was visible through a thin section of bars. Outside
her cell appeared a hideously deformed Gvort. His head
looked as though it had been held in front of a plasma
torch. The reptilian skin of the Gvort's face had been
charred and then grafted with ill-matching patches of
thicker skin.

His left arm was twisted and broken.

"So, you are the new Human Guadda has acquired."

Akima looked at the particularly ugly Gvort and debated whether or not to talk to him. The creature smiled, revealing damaged teeth, too.

"No need to speak, Human. I am Narno. We will have much time to discuss our personal details. You will be on the stand tomorrow, and I will purchase you."

The Gvort indicated his deformed arm. "You see, I have a love of Humans. Several of them gave me this arm—and this face—to indicate their displeasure with their status as my property."

The alien let Akima take this in. "I take great pleasure in returning the favor whenever I can. Sleep well tonight, Human. And remember my name so you will know your new master when he appears to claim you tomorrow."

He flashed the bad-toothed smile again and walked away.

She stood and began looking over her cell again. Maybe there was some way to bust out of here. She was damned if she was going to wind up the victim of that creature. . . .

After another half hour looking over the hinges and bars in her cell, the pilot concluded that her first analysis had been right. There was no way out.

Well then; I'll fight until they shoot me.

No way she was going to go with that Gvort. Akima sat down and looked at the floor of her cell.

Sure. Like they haven't had to deal with that before.

"No!" another part of her brain cried. "That's how they beat you! Don't give up!"

But she was tired, very tired now. How was she going to get out of here?

You're not.

Even her subconscious was working against her.

Akima looked down at the floor and put her hands on her forehead. So much for helping Humanity. She'd had a chance. . . .

I hope Cale makes it.

All at once there was a commotion outside of her cell. Akima looked outside, but at first could see nothing. And then Korso came walking along the hallway.

"This is it, guys!" he called back over his shoulder.

"Korso?" Akima said, not quite believing it.

"How's it going, pilot?" said the captain rather casually.

"You have no *idea* how bad a day I've had."

Stith and Preed ambled up. The Mantrin pulled an energy weapon out of concealment and blasted the lock to Akima's cell.

Immediately a Klaxon began to blare.

"Where's Cale?"

"I think the Drej still have him," she said. "How did you find me?"

"Let's discuss that later, shall we?"

Preed asked, "Do you suppose this alarm has gone . . . ah, un*noticed*, Captain?"

Akima dove through the door of the cell and grabbed Stith's gun.

"*I'll* give 'em something to notice."

Akima sighted along the weapon, putting all of her concentration for a moment on targeting. All the cell doors were in line down the corridor. She leaned close to her own door and fired—*szzzp!*

There was a huge—*clunk*—as locks all along the corridor fell to the floor. She'd got them all. Akima shouted down the hallway. "Go *on,* get the hell outta here!"

Immediately prisoners flooded the hallway. It looked like it would be an effective cover to help them escape.

In fact, it looked like they might have *trouble* getting past all the traffic.

From Preed. "Well, Akima, no one can fault your marksmanship, but perhaps you might have waited until we were at the *other* end of the corridor, hmm?"

"It was a fine shot, a fine shot, pay no attention to him," Stith said.

Korso shook his head. "Shut up, Preed. Come on Akima, let's go find Cale."

Yes.

—17—

C ale stared at the walls of his cell, watching the patterns of energy. He'd first noticed them after the Drej had brought him back.

He was angry. He was depressed. Akima had been *discarded. Pop!* Ejected through the wall and right out into space. . . .

So he'd thrown a tantrum, striking out at the walls, trying to hit through them, to *escape* to get *even*. The walls had seemed the same as before, even though he *knew* he'd just been through them. None of his blows had had an effect. It had all been a big waste of time and effort. It hadn't made him feel any better.

It hadn't brought Akima back.

She was gone, and he had a lot of trouble with that. He wanted to cry. But he wasn't going to cry.

He was going to make the freakin' Drej pay!

Sitting here now, his breath coming hard, his heart beating fast, and sweat still running into his eyes, he saw a *flicker*. He stared at the wall out of the corner of his eye. It was as if there were shimmery wires *in* it, glowing across the top.

Fascinated, he watched until he thought he saw a blue line of energy slide across the wall. Could it be a locking mechanism? He'd reached out and touched it—

"Ow!"

The shock had been more surprising than painful, and it gave him a direction: Now he had a puzzle to work on.

Cale had always been good at figuring out how to make things work. It was an innate talent, almost intuitive. It had bugged the hell out of Tek.

He remembered a time, years before the alien lost his sight, that Tek was working on an energy distributor for one of the catch arms on Tau-14. Tek had sat tracing circuits on the device for hours.

Cale wanted to have his mentor come to see his designs for a spaceship on his bedroom comp. "Not now, Cale, I have to finish this," Tek had said.

"You mean when you're done, you'll come look?" the boy had asked.

"Yes, when I'm done, I'll come look."

Cale had walked over to the distributor and stared at it. Almost immediately he'd noticed a hairline fracture on a component. "Try looking at that," he'd said.

Tek had harumphed and said something about little Humans who tried to complicate things. Impatient, Cale grabbed a component meter and scanned the chip. A dull red NOT FUNCTIONING flashed across the screen and Tek had just stared, speechless.

Without another word, they'd gone to see Cale's spaceship designs.

Cale smiled at the memory. And then smiled at himself that he was suddenly finding memories of drab old Tau-14 and Tek *comforting.*

Next thing you know, I'll be wanting to reunite with Po and Firrikash.

Again, he turned his attention to the walls.

There was a cascade of various energy lines, he could see now. Concentric circles of barely visible flickers pulsed on the wall in front of him.

Aha!

He could almost see . . . yes, there was pattern! There was a timing, a rhythm to it. And based on the pattern, a locus as well. . . .

He took his hand and reached out to the wall. Again, as he touched the blue pattern of energy, there was a shock. But this time he persisted. He *had* to be right, it *had* to work. For Akima. For everyone.

His hand began to sink into the wall.

Got it!

Not willing to lose any ground, he pushed his other hand into the wall near the first. Again there was a shock, but he was ready for it. He sank his arm in to his wrist and then began to bring his hands together. Maybe if he could join them—

There was a steady resistance from the pattern, but finally his hands touched. The energy around his wrists altered, turned red, and as his hands made contact, there was a rippling effect as red radiated out from the contact point. The whole wall was red now.

Cale found he could move his arms with no shock and no resistance.

It's open.

He stepped through the wall.

"Gotcha! You hunchers don't know who you're messing with."

Cale's first step found him in the corridor. He put his foot down and started to pull his other leg through. It was stuck.

Apparently the openings closed real fast.

No problem, I'll just do it again.

And then he heard footsteps coming from around the corner just ahead. Not casual walking steps, but *marching* steps.

Uh-oh.

Cale began tugging furiously.

Come on, foot! Gotta go, or we're right back in there! C'mon, c'mon—!

At what had to be the last possible instant, Cale managed to free his foot from the wall. He ran away from the marching footsteps. There was a turn ahead, and he took it. The corridor he'd stepped into was long and straight—there was no way he could get far enough down it to avoid being seen by the time the marchers arrived. He started moving along it anyway and discovered something that seemed almost like a ladder, though it wasn't quite one a human would ordinarily use. It appeared to be going into some kind of utility chute.

Well, any port in a solar storm.

Up he went. He crouched inside the chute, panting.

After a few minutes the footsteps passed, and he looked down.

All clear.

Now that he was out of the cell, he had to get moving and find a way *off* the mothership. Fast, too, because they might decide to check on his cell at any time, reread the map or something.

Cale jumped down just in time to see another Drej morph out of the floor to join the marching group that had just passed. The Drej must have felt some vibration or something because he started to turn around.

Crap!

Cale ducked behind a support beam near the wall, and the Drej didn't see him.

He turned and headed the other way. The corridors looped and twisted, and every moment was an adreneline-filled rush. Several times Cale heard Drej approach; luckily each time he was able to duck or double back.

Eventually he noticed another of the up-and-down utility tubes.

Maybe there is another way around this hulk.

Since the majority of the Drej seemed to morph through walls when they wanted to change levels, he probably wouldn't run into any of them climbing ladders—or so he hoped. And thinking about it, he had to wonder: If they could move through walls, why would there even *be* ladders on this tub?

Well, he could worry about that later.

He began to climb. Eventually, he found himself above the huge audience chamber he'd been in earlier. The crawl space seemed to lead to repair of the lighting for the room below. The huge Drej that had appeared in the sphere projection earlier was in the room on the raised platform.

It was saying something. He turned the translator's pickup toward the creature:

"—so we must prepare forces to destroy the *Titan*. Should the bioform Humans regain control of it, we must be prepared to enact plans for final elimination of the species."

Great. Things just keep on getting better, *don't they?*

The urgency he'd felt since getting out of his cell went up ten notches. He had to get out of here and *warn* people. Cale dropped down the utility chute and started running down the nearest corridor.

Got to find a ship.

But what he found instead, of course, were more Drej.

Their leader's speech had set things in motion. As he watched, a bunch of them started to morph up through the floor of the corridor ahead. To his right was what looked like another utility chute, only this one went down.

Cale dove for it just as the first Drej completed their trip through the wall.

When he hit the bottom of the tube—landing on his stomach, naturally—he found himself in a hangar.

Perfect, he had time to think, just as he noticed a stinger ship coming down from above. As the ship neared the floor of the hangar, a Drej pilot morphed through the bottom of the craft and marched away. Fortunately he was facing away from Cale as he did so.

He saw where another stinger was going to land on the hangar floor and rolled in that direction. When the ship landed, he'd be in a perfect spot to work the trick that opened Drej walls and get into the stinger. He hoped.

The ship moved lower and lower, and all at once, Cale noticed that there were no landing gear on this particular stinger.

Which meant he was about to become squished Cale sandwich with stinger on top. He started looking for the energy patterns on the ship. He was going to have much less time than he'd thought to work on this—

The ship was almost on him now. Cale felt himself tense as he tried the opening technique. There were the patterns. . . .

The floor began to open under him. Ah, shit! Must be some kind of automated maintenance program to go lower, to a repair bay or maybe storage.

He started to fall through the dissolving wall, the stinger right on top of him.

Oh, man—! "Come on, come on, come *on—!*"

He had the pattern, there, right there! He could *do* this!

And then the trick worked again, and he was *in*, at the controls.

Whew!

The controls weren't like anything he had ever seen before, but there were only so many ways an organism with arms could operate it. Cale found a stick and what looked like switches to activate propulsion. What the hell, he didn't have a lot to lose. Cale pressed a button and the ship started to hum. At least it hadn't blown up.

Yeah, well, that's only the first button, right?

–18–

Susquehana, Queen of the Drej, stood in her personal chamber tasting the warm glow of victory.

I have it!

She had succeeded where others had failed. The young biobod Cale Tucker had been traced to Sesharrim, where he had been obtained along with a biobod companion. Perhaps a—what did the biobods call it—friend? Such an alien concept, personal loyalty before the race. Sickening. It was of no consequence—the extra biological had been . . . expelled.

The Queen considered how well events were flowing. She had the map, and along with it, a clear direction to the *Titan*. She would obtain the ship, discover any technology that could be of use to the Drej, and then destroy the vessel. Where there were no pieces for an enemy to benefit from, there could be no benefit.

But there were risks. Her *droheh* had easily extrapolated the position of the *Titan* from the information on the human's hands. The biobod had been among others of his kind for a long period of time before he had been captured. The biobods were slow and stupid, but given enough time, even they could stumble onto hidden meanings.

She considered the possibility that the biologicals had *also* calculated where the *Titan* could be. Her mind rushed along path after path, permutations of possibilities.

It all came down to the same thing: If the biobods controlled the *Titan*, it would not bode well for her race. Even without Drej-comparable technology, possession of the ship alone could rally the humans to a better position. Any position other than the one they now possessed was *not* of benefit.

Much energy could be conserved allowing an enemy race to die out through what the biologicals called a "broken spirit." The Drej had seen it happen before: take away the past, disable the present, and biobods grew weaker until there were fewer and fewer paths for them to tread.

So far the Drej conquest of this galaxy had been slow. Eliminating race home worlds one at a time let other races believe they would not be destroyed and created dissension between the survivors and those who risked helping them. It took too much energy to destroy a planet, forcing the Drej to spend time recovering. And it need be a tricky business—if the other races knew before the deed was far enough along, it might cause problems. Eventually, of course, even the biologicals would realize they were being eliminated. But by that day there would be colonies across the galaxy, with enough firepower to match the rest of the beings who might consider challenging them.

Part of the myth cultivated by the Queens was that the Drej did not fail. A race that had been defeated *stayed* defeated. If the Humans were to regain a world, the myth of Drej invincibility would be shaken.

And if the Humans did manage to regain control of the *Titan*, and there *were* elements of Artifact technology. . . .

They would be dangerous in ways the Drej had not yet faced.

Not *what I would wish my legacy to be.*

DANGER TO THE RACE

No. The Orb—

PREPARE ALTERNATES TO CURRENT STRATEGY

Yes, of course. I had already considered—

CONCUR

The danger from the *Titan* almost outweighed its benefit. If there was the slightest chance that the Humans could use it to *hurt* the race, then other strategies must be readied. Susquehana had known this to be the case, but the Orb did not balance risk as she did. That was not its function.

Inastalah cohaj Drej. Together we round the race.

It was a phrase she'd heard often from her predecessor. A thought came to the Queen then—how many times had her predecessors been "rounded" in the midst of a particular stratagem? Could the destruction of the Human home world have been such threat management by the Orb? That event had destroyed the then-Queen.

The thought that followed was as clear as new starlight.

If the Orb can cause strategy to precipitate succession, I must be careful indeed.

Susquehana activated a control and opened a link to Fantiquar in communications. "Call *droheh* leaders for *inorstalla* within the next *benhah* and cause our agents among the bioforms to make ready data on the Human infestation."

Fantiquar nodded at her projection high over his head. "As you wish, my Queen."

Susquehana inclined her head at her communications leader. "Yes. *Inastalah cohaj Drej.*"

He looked confused for a moment as to the last; no matter. Let him think *he* helped round the race.

The Queen prepared for her trip to the meeting chamber. In a public instructional meeting such as the one she was going to, she was permitted to attend armed. The sheer number of possible attackers allowed the custom.

She mounted a series of double focus-burners on her limbs. After her public execution of the recent plotters she did not expect trouble.

Did I expect it, there would be triple-burners.

There was much she had to relate to her *droheh.* The last quarter *benhah* had been spent planning extermination of the remainder of the Human race. It was a step she would prefer not to take; it was wasteful to expend energy when they would surely die out within a few generations.

However, as the Orb indicated, risk to Drej domination of this galaxy predicated certain strategic backups.

Destruction of the Humans would create victory down either path should the biobods take control of *Titan.* If the ship contained no dangerous technology, destruction of all Humans would remove the status of *Titan* as a rallying point, as there would be no one left to call forth. On the other limb, if the ship were dangerous, destruction of the Humans would effect the same end, with perhaps more difficulty. Two problems with one solution, Drej efficiency in action.

The Queen glowed brighter at the thought.

The main problem in her plans had been figuring out *how* to exterminate the rest of the species. The act itself was not a problem; biobods were easy to extinguish. No, the problem was that they were so spread out. Some of them lived with other species, and there was a risk to attacking such enclaves: no single race could defeat the *Drej*, of course, but should a *number* of races be stirred against the Drej, then expansion would slow, and perhaps halt for a time.

This would be bad.

The Queen had used her communications experience from before taking the Orb to calculate how to separate the humans from the other biologicals. Bioforms were all disgustingly factionalized, all denying their similarities to focus on interspecies—and even *same* species—differences, she had remembered. This was nothing like the unity of the Drej, and it was a weakness that she could exploit.

Attacks would be launched at the primary, purely Human colonies. There were not very many of these, only a few thousand, and they would easily be destroyed by a few dozen *slijah* ships each. The attacks would be simultaneous and deliberately brutal. This would create a tension between the races that harbored the remaining scattered Humans and their guests.

The Drej would then send messages to the biobod hosts suggesting that they release their Human visitors who were needlessly endangering them. Based on the histories of some of the biobods she'd studied, the Queen was sure that this process would be hastened if the messages indicated that the Humans had *earned* the Drej wrath they were receiving.

Biological factionalism would do the rest. The Humans would be expelled from their hiding places and sent into space—where they would die.

CONCUR

She looked at the timedial on the console before her.

It was time to leave for the meeting chamber. There, she would share the plan with her *droheh*, who would lead the attack teams if the strategy were needed.

The Queen searched the corridor outside her chamber with the eyes of nearby drones. There appeared to be no danger, but as Queen there was no need to take chances.

The race was depending on her.

The meeting was over.

Susquehana waited until the majority of the assembled *droheh* had departed before making her exit. There were two schools of thought on this—if she left ahead of the crowd she would put her back to them, which she despised. On the other limb, leaving *after* gave them time to prepare an ambush.

When the chamber had cleared, she descended the speaking platform and made her way toward the main exit. As she neared the portal door, two drones moved rapidly through it toward her.

Without thinking, she fired three of the focus-burners at the one on the right. He exploded in a satisfying hiss and the other drone fell to the floor as well, putting his head low into the darkness of his shadow, a show of drone submission.

Her fingers stilled on the firing studs of the focus-burners. One part of her visual awareness maintained target lock on the living drone, another took the eyes of a drone in the hallway ahead and scanned for other dangers, while yet a third grabbed an inanimate viewing point high on the chamber wall. No one would surprise her anytime soon.

"I humbly offer *hamaj* to you, my Queen. I did not intend—"

No, he probably had not. "What is your designation?"

"I am Iliahan, *droheh* sub-prime from navigation."

"What urgency propelled you near death?"

"My Queen, the human has escaped!"

Escaped?

"We were examining the precise termination of the map vector in the nebula and decided to run another holo-extrapolation, but when we checked the holding pen the human was gone!"

Susquehana ran her own checks as she stood there. Indeed, the human's cell had been vacated. Well, he had been but an afterthought. Wait—what had Iliahan said after he'd announced the escape—"examining the precise termination?"

"And you are now *not sure* you have a termination vector for the *Titan?*"

The drone's head dipped even lower.

Fargh.

"What is the error variance on the current extrapolation?"

"Approximately a light month, my Queen."

Well, it could be worse.

"Take us to the existing termination. We will find it."

And then Susquehana indicated the still-smoking drone near Iliahan. "Was this another member from navigation?"

The drone shook his head. "No, my Queen, he was not. We spoke briefly as we awaited the termination of the *inorstalla*. He was from engineering and only said he had urgent news about the shielding project."

Fargh, again. The dark half of fortune never shadows partially.

Susquehana nodded to herself. It was an honored aphorism that these events happened in threes. She wasn't looking forward to the third.

–19–

Akima didn't really feel rescued until they were clear of the atmosphere, and then only barely.

The bridge felt tighter than usual: Gune was at the sensors and Stith had settled down behind the little alien, impatient to *do* something. After spending time alone in a cell, the pilot was glad for the company.

She and Gune had worked the nav console, backtracking the path of the Drej mothership. Akima had been lucky with a capital *L*.

The *Valkyrie* had been trailing the stinger ships that had captured her and Cale on Sesharrim when they had come across the Gvort's slave ship. Korso had hailed the slaver and inquired about Drej in the vicinity. The ship, heavily armed as most slavers were, had responded with a warning shot from a laser cannon and a brief message telling the *Valkyrie* to back off or risk being salvaged and added to the other slaves it had collected.

Gune had dropped a marker beacon at the meeting point and Korso had followed the Gvort ship at maximum sensor distance on the off chance that she and Cale had been picked up. He'd been half right.

If he hadn't taken the chance. . . .

She didn't want to think about that.

Akima's hands played over the controls, glad for their solid familiarity. They'd reached the marker beacon about a half hour ago, and had taken the heading she'd noted as she floated in the cocoon.

She was torn between wanting to travel faster to catch up with Cale, and not wanting to miss any other cocoons that might have been ejected from the ship. She hoped that if he'd been ejected it had been much later—otherwise his air supply. . . .

To hell with it. She pulled the throttle back. *Let's get there faster.*

"Gune, you see anything yet? The cocoon I was in was nonmetallic."

"No, no, nothing like that," said the little alien. "Ah—but, well, there *is* a Drej ship approaching—"

"What?!"

Stith was already up and moving toward the auxiliary weapons control. "I am on it. Come to Stith, fools."

Akima commed Korso. "Looks like we've got a problem up here, boss."

The captain must have been on his way to the bridge because he walked in within a few seconds of her call. "Problem? What problem?"

At that moment the stinger shot past the *Valkyrie*. The aft scanner showed it slowing. It turned around.

"Okay, Stith, do your thing!" Korso activated an ancillary console near navigation and called up gunnery.

"One ship. One shot," Stith said. "Not to worry."

"Gune—any sign of his buddies?"

"No, there is only the one. He is all alone."

That's odd.

From Stith, "I'm locked on—die, Drej fool." She fired.

• • •

Cale had had better days. Lots of them. In fact, given his current situation, all the bad days he'd had before seemed downright pleasant.

The escape had gone better than he could have hoped, but trying to operate the stinger was frustrating.

He'd played with the throttle and attitude controls until he felt confident enough to move, and the next time a squad of stingers had launched, he'd joined the formation and split off before they knew he'd been with them.

Unfortunately, navigation had never been his strong suit; once he'd gotten away, he had no idea where to go. He didn't even know *where* he was.

He'd figured that the *Valkyrie* might be tracking the mothership, so he lined himself up with its path and headed in the exact opposite direction.

With any luck—okay, a *lot* of luck—he might run into them. . . .

Sure, if you don't run out of fuel first. Or starve. Or miss them at the outside of sensor range.

He'd spent a lot of time trying to figure out the rest of the stinger's controls. He *thought* he'd gotten sensors operating. After toggling a few switches, a heads up display had showed his ship heading away from a larger dot. The mothership, he hoped.

After several hours he caught a blip on the sensors. Was there any way to do a better scan? Probably, but he sure couldn't figure out what it was. Looked like the only way to get a better look was to use the old 20/20 scanners. He noted his current heading and altered course toward the blip.

Cale peered out of the cockpit's ports as he neared the other craft. Hmm. It looked familiar, but he couldn't be sure.

And then he was.

The Valkyrie*!*

He'd been flying so fast he quickly overshot. Cale yanked the attitude control up and executed a tight loop to head back toward the ship. He felt like cheering.

And then a panel he'd not noticed before lit up in a particularly garish red. It flashed at him and he heard a whisper of sound.

What the hell?

It was the translator. He must have turned the volume down as he got into the stinger. He tabbed the control back up.

"<<—ning, weapons lock on dorsal burner array. Evasive maneuvering. Warning—>>"

Oh, shit. They're going to shoot *me!*

"HEY! It's *me*! Don't shoot!" Panic drove the words out of him.

Sure, they'll hear that. *Gotta* do *something—*

Communications, communications, where were the damn communications? Cale had studiously avoided anything that could have been a comms control, not wanting to alert the Drej to the fact that he'd stolen one of their ships.

He'd just have to hope they weren't listening right now.

He began punching buttons all over the console, anything that looked like it could be used to talk to someone. Green, red, blue—he activated them all.

"<<Weapons arrays activated.>>"

Oh, no! Didn't need the Valkyrie *seeing that* right now*.

Reaching across to activate a large purple button, he accidentally jerked the attitude controls.

This was lucky; the ship tumbled just as a plasma bolt

from the *Valkyrie* passed through the space he had vacated.

Pushing the purple button had done *something* however. He heard control voices. *Drej* voices, but voices.
If the *Valkyrie* was monitoring. . . .

Code. Use a code so the Drej wouldn't know—

"Three . . . five . . . twenty-two . . ."

Akima sent the *Valkyrie* into a high parabola relative to
their previous course. The Drej had activated weapons.
Well, one of them wasn't going to be enough. Stith
would cook the bastard, even if the pilot of this particular little ship was good. Akima had to give him that.
He'd dodged the plasma burst Stith had fired with expert
timing.

"I missed," Stith said. It was in as incredulous a tone
as she might have used in speaking as a witness to the
heat-death of the universe.

Gune, who had been muttering some numbers, tapped
Akima on the shoulder. "It's Cale, I think."

Cale?

"Cale?"

"Yes, a code—"

Korso picked up on it faster. "Stith! Hold your fire—"

But it was too late. The Mantrin fired another plasma
burst, and then turned to Korso. "Oops."

The stinger had managed to dodge the plasma bolt.

"It must be Cale," Stith said. "No Drej could avoid
two of my shots."

"Akima, open the cargo bay."

Akima tabbed the appropriate controls and slowed the
ship. The stinger immediately slowed as well, matching
velocity, and arced toward the cargo bay.

Akima put the ship on autopilot and headed for the
cargo bay, two steps ahead of the others.

●   ●   ●

As soon as he could hear the hissing of air outside the stinger, Cale did his trick with the bottom of the Drej ship and popped out on the floor.

The door to the cargo bay popped open, and Akima came running over.

"Cale!"

His heart seemed to thump an extra beat. She was alive!

He reached out to hug her as she extended her hand to shake. Before they could match arms, however, the rest of the crew crowded around them.

Gune smiled, his thick glasses reflecting the overhead lights of the cargo bay in Cale's eyes. "The boy is *not* dead! This is cause for happiness. And look what he has brought us!"

From the way Gune looked at the stinger ship, Cale wasn't sure if he was happier about his escaping, or the chance to dissect the Drej vessel. But who cared?

Preed was noncommittal as usual. "Hmm."

From Akima. "So how did you escape?"

Preed cut in. "He got lucky."

You don't know the half of it, Preed.

Korso stepped forward next, smiling. He looked pleased. "You know, we were just about to rescue you."

Cale looked at the older man. He seemed serious.

"Yeah? Well, thanks."

Korso nodded. "Anytime."

The map—I'd better tell him.

"Look, they copied the map. I'm sure they're heading for the *Titan* now."

Korso didn't seem worried. "They won't find it." He turned to the others. "Stations, people."

The crew headed for their posts.

"Akima—"

She stopped.

"What happened? I mean—I thought you were—how did you get back?"

She smiled and looked into his eyes. "Got picked up with the trash. Luckily, Korso got there before I wound up as the door prize."

There was a glimmer of some deeper emotion there. Cale wanted to hear the rest of that story.

He reached out and brushed a lock of hair from her face. "I guess I owe him one."

She smiled again, and he could feel the connection. "Ah—you know, we both got pretty lucky back there. But the next time—"

Korso cut in. "Cale, come on!" He indicated the map tattoo. "Gune needs a hand!"

Cale looked over his shoulder at Akima.

Later.

—20—

Cale stood in Gune's lab and shifted back and forth, trying to get comfortable as the little alien twisted his wrist to look at the map.

Ow!

"Hey, take it easy!"

Even the Drej hadn't twisted his arm *this* much.

Gune, oblivious as usual, carried on. "Yes, the map *is* good. But it is *different. Clear* now. Very much the case."

Different?

Cale looked over his shoulder, craning his neck to see what the little alien was talking about. Sure enough, there *was* a difference. Part of the tattoo was . . . pulsing.

"Hey, what's it doing?"

"Ahhh," said Preed, nodding. "The distal phalangeal meridian."

Cale glared at the alien. Distal *what*?

"Okay, Gune," asked Korso, "what does it *mean*?"

"The Ice Rings of Tigrin. Right here, past the outer quadrant." Gune pointed, somehow twisting Cale's arm even more.

The boy shifted, attempting yet again to keep his joints from breaking.

Surprisingly strong, Gune was.

Preed chimed in. "Easy to get lost out there."

"But a good hiding place," Korso said. "Looks like we're one step ahead of the Drej after all, kid."

But Cale didn't say anything. After the Drej ship, Korso could call him whatever he wanted to.

Korso looked at Gune. "You're *sure* about the location?"

"Yes, Captain, this time I'm absolutely sure," said Gune. "At least unless the map changes again."

"Then I guess we're back in business."

Cale found himself walking toward the bridge after Gune had finished his map inspection. He hadn't really had a chance to see the control layout on the trip to Sesharrim and thought it might give him some ideas for his next ship design.

And that's the only reason you want to go to the bridge?

Well . . . in a word, no. Akima was there.

He still found it hard to believe she was alive. It was such a relief.

So he was disappointed when he got to the bridge and no one was there. The *Valkyrie* could, of course, be controlled from any console on the ship, so there didn't *need* to be anyone there, but it seemed odd to find it empty.

He stared out the kleersteel panels in front of the pilot's position. It was comfortable, just staring for a change. No worrying about being caught by Drej.

Something shimmery floated past the cockpit port, followed by another something, then another—a whole slew of somethings. Cale peered closer and realized that dozens of some kind of *creature* were flying around just outside the *Valkyrie*. They were almost transparent, and he had to strain to see them. Were they dangerous? Should he call someone? What were they?

From behind him came Korso's voice. "They're called wake angels. They follow ships in deep space and glide on the energy wake. Nobody knows where they come from. Supposed to be good luck, so they say."

Cale leaned forward to see the angels better. They were gorgeous. Like the Drej, they seemed to radiate light, but there was no possibility of mistaking one for the other. The Drej were frightening, their light like some kind of effect from a horror-holo, while these seemed to glow like the stars.

"They're almost like ghosts."

Korso had come forward so he could see the creatures as well. He indicated the pilot's chair. "Why don't you give them some wake to follow?"

Fly the Valkyrie*? Korso is going to let me fly the Valkyrie?*

"You sure about that?"

"What's the worst thing that could happen? You kill us all, right?"

Trying not to look too eager, Cale eased himself into the pilot's chair and gripped the flight control levers.

Better take it slow to start.

He wasn't too worried about his ability to handle the ship—after all, he'd taught himself to fly a Drej stinger. But if he didn't take it easy, Korso might change his mind.

He eased the throttle back, just enough to indicate he'd taken control, and altered the course fractionally to starboard. The controls were more sensitive than he'd expected, and there was a slight wobble as the ship registered his hand movements.

Korso seemed to relax. "Yeah, you've got it. Go on,

open her up a bit. Let's give these creatures something to *chase*."

Cale glanced over at Korso. Still calm. The boy snapped the throttle up from the nominal 25 percent they'd been running to over 50 percent. A giant hand seemed to squeeze him against the padded fit-foam of the pilot's chair, and he saw Korso's knuckles go white as the older man grabbed on to the console control.

"Chase *this*, guys."

The angels dove to get out of the way of the suddenly accelerated *Valkyrie* and Cale followed easily, keeping pace with the shimmery creatures. He slapped the attitude control lever to the right, hard, and rolled the ship over before shooting high above the course they'd been following, like a missile taking off.

The angels were fast, almost as fast as the *Valkyrie*, and he watched them close on the ship. Cale increased the throttle.

They were in a gas field now, probably with some iron oxide mixed in, and he had to steer around giant streamers that looked like columns of red fog.

This was a real *blast*!

Korso was less relaxed now. "Uh, Cale— Be careful of the— Watch it!"

A wake angel shot in front of the ship and nearly became a smashed angel, but Cale popped left, missing it.

"Whooeee!" This was great fun.

Both men laughed at the near miss. Cale took the ship on a few more fast climbs and dives before throttling back. Korso helped correct to their previous course.

"Thank you," Cale said.

Korso shrugged. "I knew you could handle this old bird."

"No," said Cale, "I mean—for trying to find me." He

was silent for a beat. "It's more than my father ever did."

Korso let out a sigh and shook his head slightly. "You still don't get it, do you? Your father was a great man, Cale. If you had stayed with him, you'd probably be long dead by now." He looked directly at him. "He would have been proud of you."

The container in his mind where he'd put all his memories of his father seemed to spring a leak. Cale had long since sealed those feelings away: Thinking about them hurt too much. As a Human in an alien world, he didn't *dare* let anyone see him hurt.

But here, he felt more relaxed than he had in ages. Maybe it was the good feelings he had about Akima, or how Korso had shown that he wasn't going to go away—he wasn't sure.

But the old emotions, including the deep desire for approval, were still there. Cale swallowed.

"You really think so?" he said, keeping his voice as flat as he could.

You think my daddy would be proud?

"Trust me."

Hold it in.

"Thanks," he managed. "You know, I miss him."

"Me, too."

And a look of pain crossed Korso's face.

I guess we all keep it inside.

The two men stared at the stars.

The nightmare woke him from a dead sleep.

In the dream, Cale had been sitting on his bunk on the *Valkyrie*. A noise had come from the hallway, and he'd turned to look as the door to his cabin slid open in that slow, deliberate way that only happens in dreams. Two Drej stood in the doorway, weapons aimed at him. Cale moved to get up, but he was too slow, way too slow. His body felt like it was moving in heavy syrup, and he could feel the Drej sighting on him.

And then they fired, blasting him across the bunk. He fell, and woke up in the same place he'd fallen in the dream.

Way, way too much, he thought as he rolled out of bed. No way he was going to try to go back to sleep yet.

He checked the wall chrono. It was a bit past eight, ship time. Something was different—

They'd stopped. At least the drive engines weren't running. The subtle vibration was gone.

When had this happened? What was going on? Unnerved by the dream and not knowing why they'd stopped, Cale stepped out into the corridor.

He walked down the corridor, intending to head to the bridge, but then stopped outside Akima's cabin. On impulse, he knocked.

There was no answer. Worried, he thumbed the door button. The door slid open. "Akima? Akima?"

She was naked. He got only a fast glimpse of her from behind as she snatched up a towel and covered herself. She had nice legs.

Well, *of course* she had nice legs. She had nice everything, didn't she?

Apparently she hadn't heard him, because she jumped. "Damn! I thought I locked that! I must be going senile."

Cale blushed. "Uh, sorry—I—"

"In or out," she said, "but shut the door."

The air in her cabin was warmer than that of the corridor, and he realized he was letting the cold in.

"Uh—in," he said, closing the door behind him.

She stood up and motioned for him to turn around. Cale did as he was asked, and he *heard* the towel she was wearing drop to the floor. He swallowed, his throat gone very dry.

She was probably *naked* right behind him.

He heard her dress, and decided he'd better say something before she realized what he was thinking.

"Any idea why we've stopped?"

Was that a reflection over there? There was a shelf with some old Earth memorabilia on it, a baseball, postcards, and some other junk. There was a chrome metal rod supporting the shelf that glinted as Akima moved behind him. Not a very good reflection, unfortunately.

"Pit stop for the basics: food, water, shield-core reactant. You know, the usual. Not much of that where we're headed."

He fidgeted.

Come on, Cale, talk!

"Where'd you get all this junk?"

Akima grabbed his shoulder from behind and turned him around. Cale's eyes went wide at her touch.

Stay cool, stay cool here.

"It's not junk. Why don't you come with me, and I'll show you?"

Sure. He'd go anywhere with her. Anywhere at all.

Cale followed her out of the cabin. "Where are we going?"

"For a tour of our rest stop," she said.

—21—

C ale walked with Akima through the drifter colony marketplace. The colony, called New Bangkok, was a study in contrasts, and the marketplace fit right in. Tables and stalls that wouldn't have been out of place in a medieval village stood on top of pitted plasteel, right next to emergency life-support stations. The stations looked exactly like the kind found on Tau-14, bubbles to run to in the event of a hull breach.

Which might be likely on a hulk like New Bangkok; like most drifter colonies, it was made up of hundreds of ships that had come from Earth and been assembled into a form for which they had never been designed.

Stranger than the look of the colony, however, were the people. Cale couldn't put his finger on it, but there was an odd air about them. They weren't particularly strange on themselves—they bustled around just like people on Tau-14. He did notice a sense of poverty to them—he saw few shipsuits that didn't have patches— but no one looked like they were starving.

And then, as he watched a group of children gathered

around an ice-cream stand, it hit him: This was a community that was made up of *Humans*. He hadn't seen more than a handful of nonhumans since they'd entered the station airlock.

We're the majority here.

Maybe that explained the lack of caution and the confidence of everyone he saw. On Tau-14, Humans were second class, always careful not to offend nonhumans lest they pay the price. Here, they didn't have to.

For as long as Cale could remember he'd been in the minority. Even during the time he'd spent on Tek's home world, being Human had meant being an outsider.

Seeing such a community was very different.

Ahead of him, Akima was picking over some odd-looking shoes. A nearby sign proclaimed FROM EARTH!

Cale moved up alongside her. "You going to get some more Earth junk?" he asked.

Akima turned to him. "You don't get it, do you Cale? This *junk* is all that's left of where we came from. It isn't just *stuff*. Each piece is a reminder of what it means to have a place—to have a *home*."

"I wouldn't know about that," he said. *Until I met you*, he wanted to add.

It was true. The more time he spent around Akima, the stronger his feelings seemed to get. It was almost as if by being near her he'd found a place to call home.

But he didn't say any of that. Instead, he just looked at her and *willed* her to know how he felt.

She shook her head and looked back down at the shoes. They looked like a pair of slippers, charcoal colored, with an odd pull-string that looked as if it were used to tighten them. She picked them up and moved over to the man who ran the stall.

Cale started to walk away when he saw a black sheath with a knife in it, almost hidden under some hats near the edge of the merchandise. He reached down and picked it up. There were chrome fittings on the leather and the smell was oddly familiar. Inside the sheath was a double-edged blade, blackened to reduce reflection.

Hmm.

"Nice selection, young man." It was the stall keeper.

"That's a replica of the Sykes-Fairbairn commando knife. Not much call for commandos these days, but it still has value as . . . oh, you know . . . a paperweight." The man winked.

Cale smiled. He liked the knife. Maybe Korso could show him how to use it. He had the impression the older man knew a lot about such things. Might be handy if he should run into some more Drej. Now there was just the question of how to pay for it.

He turned and saw Akima smiling at him.

Who wants old junk now? Her expression seemed to say.

He smiled back. *Got me.*

He didn't have any money, but when they left the market he had a new paperweight, courtesy of Akima.

The trip back to the *Valkyrie* was pleasant and uneventful—two words Cale was finding more and more attractive.

He was anxious to show Korso his new knife and wanted to head immediately for the captain's quarters. Akima wanted to drop off her purchases, so they stopped by her cabin first. It didn't occur to either of them to separate.

As they neared Korso's cabin, they could hear him talking to someone. He must have left his door open. Cale looked at Akima and winked. Just what Korso needed to wake him up, a visit from Cale Tucker, super commando. She smiled.

Korso's voice was louder now.

"You think this is some kind of *game*? We had a *deal*, dammit! How *dare* you try to cut me out!"

Akima and Cale exchanged a glance. Who was Korso talking to?

They moved closer. Cale didn't want to eavesdrop, but his curiosity was getting the better of him. And then he heard it. The voice. *That* voice.

"We will do as we please in order to insure the retrieval of the *Titan*. Do not presume to limit us, Human. We are Drej."

The alien queen. It was *her*.

Akima looked as shocked as Cale felt.

Man! Korso was dealing with the Drej!

Cale felt as if he had been kicked in the stomach. He couldn't even breathe.

Korso went on. "Do as you please, and guess what? You'll retrieve *nothing*. You don't have the *whole* map. The kid's got it, and *I've* got the kid. So you keep your drones off my ass, or so help me, *I'll rip his heart out*. And I'll burn his hand to ash!"

There was an inarticulate snarl from the other voice, and the chime of a discom.

Holy shit!

Akima was the first to move.

"Cale, come on!" she whispered.

They turned to leave and ran right into Preed, standing behind them with his gun already out.

"Going somewhere? Mmm—no, I think not."

Cale and Akima stared at him. "That way," he said, waving his gun at Korso's cabin.

"Who's there?"

"Look what I found, Captain! Two little birdies. With big ears."

Korso shook his head. He managed to look a little

guilty, but not enough. "How much did you hear?"

"Enough," said Akima. "You bastard!"

Cale said, " 'Trust me' you said. You *lied*! Everything you said, everything you told me."

Korso had the grace not to play guilty. "Not everything. Your father *did* hide a ship. And the Drej killed him. All because he couldn't face the truth."

"And what truth might that be?"

"The Human race is out of gas, kid. It's finished. The only thing that matters—if you're smart—is getting what you can before someone else beats you to it."

Cale remembered when he'd said nearly the same thing to Tek. Get what you can. But now he knew better. There *was* more. The feeling of community he'd seen in the market, the feelings he had for Akima.

"No. You're wrong. I used to believe that, but not anymore."

"Well, then, I guess you're even more like your father than I thought. *He* was a fool, too."

Cale lost it. No way he was going to listen to this traitor call *his* father a fool! He dove forward and slammed into Korso, his momentum taking them both to the floor. Akima moved, but Preed grabbed her.

A mistake on Preed's part.

Akima hammered the Akrennian, smacked him right in the face, and knocked him back. He was stunned—but not down.

"Cale!"

He rolled up and away from Korso.

"Come on, Cale! Go!"

Korso yelled at Preed, "Stay on 'em! I'll lock it down."

This was bad. If he locked the ship down, they would be trapped, no way on or off.

Akima was almost to the doorway.

"Go! Go!" Cale called out to her.

Preed was already moving to cut her off, though. There wasn't much time left. Cale looked desperately for a weapon. He'd dropped the knife in the scuffle with Korso and couldn't see it.

What could he use?

The drink machine! He slapped the refill control and hot, green liquid hissed and burbled and started pouring into a cup.

Cale grabbed the cup before it had completely filled and tossed it at Korso. The hot, green beverage splashed all over the older man's face.

"Ahhh!"

Try locking things down now, *pervo!*

Preed had reached Akima, but stopped at Korso's yell. Just in time for Cale to butt him in the stomach.

"Ooooff." Preed went down.

Cale and Akima ran down the corridor toward the airlock. He heard footsteps behind them and realized that the Akrennian had recovered enough to follow them.

Seems like I spend a lot of time running down damned corridors.

The boy took a quick glance over his shoulder. Preed had his gun, and Korso was just coming out of his quarters.

Oh, crap!

But they reached the exit and barreled out of the ship.

Akima was just ahead, so Cale saw her when Preed shot her. She went down hard, collapsing on the deck.

Cale ran to her. She was still breathing, but it didn't look good. He looked back at Preed. If looks could have killed, Preed would have been a smoking hole in the floor.

Preed smiled then, and it seemed to Cale to be the most honest emotion he'd yet seen from the alien. The

Akrennian pointed his gun at Akima. He made a show of slowly aiming the pistol.

"Say good-bye to your girlfriend, Human."

The world seemed to go silent and slow.

"Hey! What's going on here?! Stop!"

Cale realized that some of the colonists were suddenly there. He saw several older women, and a couple of middle-aged men. They moved to shelter Akima from Preed's fire.

Cale was touched. What he'd seen before, in the marketplace, had been the tip of the iceberg. Not only were humans the majority on New Bangkok, but they also took care of their own.

Preed was going to have to shoot them all.

The wiry alien grinned. He must have reached the same conclusion—and it didn't seem bother him in the least. "Cook one, cook a dozen, no difference," he said. He extended the gun.

Korso stepped in and grabbed Preed's gun. "Leave it," Cale heard him say. "They don't matter. We have what we need."

A long moment passed. Preed lowered the gun. "You're all history anyhow," he said.

Korso and Preed vanished into the ship.

Cale looked down at Akima. She smiled, a weak one—and then her eyes rolled up to show nothing but white.

Akima!

–22–

Cale's opinion of humans on New Bangkok continued to rise after Korso and Preed fled with the ship.

Several colonists helped him carry Akima along a crowded sidewalk. They moved across the market square and through an older section of the habitat. Graffiti decorated the walls and ceilings; one piece in particular seemed to stand out. It was a golden orb with a question mark inscribed in its center. What did that mean?

An old woman who looked to be Asian, something Akima had said she was, indicated a large round table ahead of them. Cale and the others carefully laid Akima down and stepped back.

Cale looked down at her. Her eyes were still closed. *Let her be all right. Please.*

It was too much. He'd finally met a girl he liked, and who—unbelievably still—seemed to like *him*. And so, naturally, she got shot.

The woman shouted something at another colonist in some kind of strange language. The syllables all seemed to go together, almost like singing.

She turned to another colonist. "You, go get doctor!"

"Yeah, and hurry!" Cale added.

Several colonists laid down some blankets. Again Cale was struck by the way that everyone seemed to be working together. He'd heard the term "community" before, but hadn't ever really known what it meant. Until now.

The old woman leaned forward and started rubbing Akima's hands. Cale remembered something about how that was supposed to help with shock. Then she looked over her shoulder at him, shook her head, and said something to a colonist in the strange language. Japanese? Chinese?

The man she'd spoken to dashed off.

"What did you say?"

"I ask him bring corn liquor."

Then Akima spoke. "No, really, I don't need it," she said, sounding very weak.

She's alive!

The old woman shook her head. "Liquor not for you, it for boy."

"Me?"

The old woman continued talking to Akima. "He pass out soon!" And then she made some kind of comment in her other language and laughed.

Cale looked at Akima. He smiled, knowing how concerned he must have looked. Some hair had fallen over her eyes and he reached down and carefully moved it aside, stroking her forehead. Her eyes closed again and she smiled and drifted off to sleep.

The first thing Akima saw when she opened her eyes was Cale, staring out a large viewport at a series of connected ships.

He must have heard her because he turned and smiled.

"Hey, Sleeping Beauty!"

"How long was I out?"

"Only a few hours—" he paused for a beat "—you had me pretty worried . . ."

Shot! I was shot!

She could feel a soreness on her right side and reached down, feeling a synthflesh patch under her arm. There seemed to be no other damage. She'd been lucky—it had missed bone and seemed to be just a minor wound.

Events started coming back to her.

"Korso and Preed—I still can't believe it! They'll get to the *Titan*. Damn."

Cale shook his head. "They won't. We're going to beat them to it."

Then he smiled a fierce smile, one she wouldn't want to be on the wrong side of. "We're going to stop them, Akima."

How long had she been asleep? Only a few *hours*? Cale seemed ready to take on the world. She rubbed her head.

"Was I hit in the head back there or something? Because it's funny—I thought you just said 'We' are gonna stop them."

"That's right."

Had he been so seriously upset that he'd warped out?

"Uh, Cale, I hate to point this out and all, but we're in the middle of nowhere, there's just the two of us, and, oh yeah, *we don't have a ship!*"

"Oh, we've got a ship. Sort of."

"Sort of?"

"Check it out."

Cale stepped back from the window and nodded toward the village of old ships. In the center was a particularly large vessel, streamlined for atmospheric landings.

It was certainly pre-AE—maybe even one of the first
deepspace ships.

"That would be our ride, right there."

Akima shook her head. "You're kidding."

While Akima had been sleeping off the medicine the
doctor had given her, Cale had been questioned by the
old Chinese woman. Cale had been so grateful for her
help that he'd leveled with her.

She'd been surprised to hear that not only was he
looking for the *Titan*, but that he knew where it was.
He'd revealed his map-palm to her, and she'd gasped.

"We always believe in *Titan*," she'd said. She'd
pointed at the orb graffiti he'd wondered about earlier.
"The question was when. Now we have answer."

She'd looked at his palm again and seemed to make
some kind of decision. "I try to get help."

So he'd waited next to Akima. To his surprise, after
only an hour or so, the woman had returned with a man
who'd said he was the mayor of the oldest section of
New Bangkok, the original ship collection. The habitat
had expanded since then, but some of the original ref-
ugee ships, which early colonists had joined with a variety of makeshift conduits and couplings, were still
there. The mayor had explained that his ship was so old
that it hadn't meshed well with the more modern majority.

"Besides," the old man had said, "I wanted to be ready
to run again—if we ever needed to."

The mayor then told Cale that he would gladly give
up his home if there was a real chance that the *Titan*
would be found.

"You don't know that this means," he'd said.

"Maybe I do," Cale had replied. "Finally."

He'd asked Cale to come see the ship, and Cale had

said he would—as soon as Akima was rested.

Now that time was here.

The mayor, a tough-looking old geep named Alex, seemed to be having second thoughts about giving up his home. Cale and Akima examined the craft as he rambled on.

"She's been a great house, but I'm not sure she'll fly." The old man looked across the cockpit at a collection of old Earth memorabila as he spoke. He seemed to be realizing just how much work it would take for him to vacate the old ship.

Cale popped open an access panel under the Drive controls.

"Well it looks like her Ionic Vacuum Drive is still intact. Those never drain."

Akima seemed . . . less than optimistic. "This thing's a wreck!"

Cale glared at her. "I can *fix* it." Then he smiled. "Of course, if you can't fly it—"

She returned the glare. "If *you* can get it to move, *I* can fly it."

It was still going to be a lot of work though. That, plus a miracle or two, maybe.

Cale stared at the wiring under the access panel. It would have to all be checked. With just him and Akima it would probably take weeks. . . .

The Chinese woman entered the room. Behind her were twenty or thirty technicians.

"I bring help."

Cale grinned. *Damn!* They might just launch this bird.

Even with all the help, it took longer than Cale would have liked. The delay put Korso ahead by two days, but it couldn't be helped. If the map changed again, of course, Korso wouldn't find it. . . .

The team of technicians worked around the clock to help Cale prepare the ship. He'd worked hard, too, and came to understand the old ship very well.

Phoenix was the name of the vessel. Cale did some checking and found out that the Phoenix was a mythological bird that was reborn from the ashes. . . .

Perfect.

Finally, it was time to go.

Cale and Akima walked up the old-style ramp of the spaceship. Colonists who'd helped them, as well as their families and friends, were all outside waving. Nervous, he'd said, "Thank you all! Thank you for coming out to the unofficial *Titan* rescue mission. Yes, I *am* the man you've heard about. Thank you! Thank you very much." He'd waved and given the crowd a thumbs-up. They had all cheered.

Then he'd said under his breath, "Okay, Cale, don't blow this . . ."

The two entered the cockpit. It was now clear of the old man's junk. It *had* been a difficult move, but he'd been happy to do it.

The two humans strapped themselves into their flight chairs.

"We're good to go," Cale said. "As good as we're gonna get."

"Let's hope she starts."

"Oh, she'll start." *Maybe blow up, too, but let's not think about that.*

"You that sure?"

"She'll start! You just better lean back for the acceleration—"

The boosters fired. There was a weak bang, followed by a series of minor explosions.

They didn't move.

"Lean back for the acceleration, you said? Maybe I should get out and push."

Cale glared at Akima, then the control panel. He kicked it. *Bastard!*

Suddenly the engines roared to life. Fire and smoke belched, and they began to move.

He looked over at Akima and gave her a told-you-so look.

She shook her head. "Okay. You did your job, now let me do mine."

The *Phoenix* moved through the maze that was the old town in New Bangkok. It took every gram of skill that Akima had as a pilot to make it work. The drive was ancient, the response was sluggish, and the handling was awful. But it was working.

Now it was Cale's turn to be nervous. He pointed at bits of debris that seemed about to collide with them.

"Uh, you see that? Don't you want to, like, *turn* to port or something? Akima?"

"Relax. I got it."

It was a rust bucket, but the *Phoenix* was in good hands. Her hands.

Ready or not, Titan, *here we come.*

—23—

They were nearing one of the Ice Rings of Tigrin when Akima spotted the *Valkyrie*. The flight had gone well—at least as well as the voyage of a ship that had been someone's *house* for over fifteen years probably could go. They kept finding old socks and other personal items in the oddest places.

There had been a few moments when she and Cale had been sure the drive might fail, but Cale managed to cobble things back together each time.

He was, she realized, quite a mechanic. He had a real feel for it.

The ice rings created sensor anomalies that made flying by instruments dangerous, so Akima had dimmed the lights in the small ship's bridge and opened all the available kleersteel port shutters. She had a panoramic view of the ice shards as they flew by. It was old-fashioned flying, her favorite type. More personal control. More danger, too, though it didn't feel like it.

Cale walked onto the bridge, behind her.

"The reflections are throwing my readings off," she said, explaining the view.

"I think we're getting closer." he said.

There was something in his voice—was he all right? She risked a quick glance over her shoulder. He was holding his hand open and staring at the map. She only saw it for an instant, but that was enough.

The map was *glowing*.

Okay, that might make me sound a little funny, too.

It was one thing to have a biokeyed map tattooed on your hand, it was another to suddenly be able to use it like a night light.

Well, maybe the change will help us pinpoint the Titan. They had reached the area where the map had said the ship was, but the ice rings were huge and spread out over a few hundred thousand miles. At least they had a head start on the Drej, who had to search the entire nebula.

Unless Korso filled them in on the latest news.

He might have, but on the other hand, from the way she'd heard him talking to the Drej it seemed like he didn't trust them. She figured he wanted to get to the *Titan* first, to be sure he would collect his money. It was probably true enough that traitors trusted nobody. Why should they?

Her awareness of the nearby ice shards was approaching what her old instructor, Porter, had like to call a "bird's-eye 360." "When you get really *in*to a flight," her instructor had told her once, "all the looking around and scanning from place to place disappears. It's like you're a bird, aware of everything around you, 360 degrees total, screens, readouts, outside, *everything*. You forget you're *looking* and just *see*."

Even so, she nearly missed the flash from the ice shard ahead. It was shaped like a giant quartz crystal and there had been something *odd* about it.

A reflection?

She did some quick mental geometry. If she'd seen a reflection coming *there* as they were approaching from *this* angle. . . .

Then there could be a ship right behind them, in the exhaust shadow. It wasn't the safest place to fly, but with a good pilot, and a strong ship, it was possible to fly in a ship's blind spot, the area behind the thrusters.

Only one way to find out.

Akima tapped the attitude control level lightly, dodging an upcoming ice spiral, and setting the ship on a collision course with a large shard maybe a minute or two distant.

She waited until it was almost too late to correct for collision and yanked the attitude control lever way up.

As she shot up the face of the ice shard, the *Valkyrie* showed up on sensors.

"Cale!"

"What?"

"It's Korso! He's right behind us!"

"Crap! We've got to lose him!"

"I hear you. Buckle up."

Akima heard the click of Cale's buckles and pushed the thruster control forward.

I hope this ship can take it.

She pushed the *Phoenix* around the edge of an ice spiral and checked the sensors. No good. The *Valkyrie* was still behind them.

Think, girl, think.

The *Valkyrie* was faster, more powerful, and had better sensors. The only thing it didn't have going for it was that *she* wasn't piloting it. Korso could fly, but not as well as she could. At least she *hoped* that was true. . . .

Phoenix had pulled away from its pursuers, but that

distance was suddenly lost. The *Valkyrie* had realized there was no point in trying to hide anymore.

A sensor screen indicated that the *Valkyrie*'s main drive had been activated. They were coming in at speed.

If they knock out our engines, we're done.

Of course they *probably* wouldn't shoot at the *Phoenix*, since she figured they still needed Cale alive.

Ahead in the distance, a pair of giant ice crystals rushed at each other in what would be a massive collision.

An idea began to form.

Just might work, too.

She accelerated toward the impending smashup.

Cale watched Akima fly.

She is so beautiful.

Seeing her pilot was a real show. She seemed to blend with the controls, making the ship a part of her, the flying almost effortless.

As much as he wanted to think he was a hotshot pilot, Cale had to admit that he would probably never be this good.

Well, at least she can't fix *things like I can.*

Not that she had to, of course, but it was nice that there was *some* balance.

She'd taken the *Phoenix* around a few shards, trying to gain some distance, but it hadn't worked. Korso and company hung on. At the moment, Akima was speeding toward a huge pair of ice shards that looked as if they were about to collide.

Bet the impact will be fantastic. Of course they couldn't sit around and watch it, what with the *Valkyrie* right behind them.

Akima throttled up a bit. Now they were moving even faster, but pretty much at the old ship's limit. Cale had flown the *Valkyrie*, no way they could outrun it.

"Can you get me some extra boost?" she asked.

Hmm. Not with the regular engines, they're maxed. Maybe with a compressed air vent, or a backup atmospheric-booster—

He was so busy thinking about the problem he lost track of their course.

When things came back into focus, a possible solution worked out, he noticed that they were even closer to the giant shards.

Abruptly he realized that they were *too* close. They were heading right into the impact zone!

I wanted to lose them, but not by leaving the land of the living to do it . . . !

He started to say so, but she cut him off.

"Do you have my boost?"

Suddenly, he could see what she was doing. At their current speed they wouldn't make it, but with a little extra—

"On its way."

Cale unbuckled himself and dove under the control panel for atmospheric engines. He knocked out the safety override.

"Try the atmospheric boost."

"Will it work?"

"Test it!"

"We don't have time."

Cale reseated himself in his chair. He understood *why* she didn't want to check it, but he was unnerved anyway. He *thought* it would work, but with mechanical things you always *checked* first!

They were on the edge of the impact zone. If they turned right now they could skim the surface of the shards and make it, but the *Valkyrie* would catch them.

Akima reached over and put her finger over the Atmospheric Boost button. "Ready?"

"Sure."

Not bad, his voice didn't even break. He had been wrong earlier. He was already a better pilot than Akima—her safety protocols left a lot to be desired.

She pushed the button.

Cale had the impression of walls closing in on both sides of their ship. Two horizons appeared on either side of the ship and were closing fast—but the extra thrust kicked in, shoving the two of them back into their seats, accelerating the *Phoenix* faster than the little ship had probably ever gone—

And all of a sudden they were *through*.

Cale watched one of the aft screens. The collision *was* impressive. And no sign of the *Valkyrie*.

"That should buy us a little time."

Cale stared at the collision. Massive chunks of shattered ice sprayed outward like a bomb. Korso would have to sheer off and fly wide to avoid the shrapnel. "Remind me not to be on the bridge next time we do that. And don't tell me, either."

She laughed.

They were inside a planetoid-sized ice fragment, inside an ice cave big enough to swallow a ship ten times as large as the one they were in. Cale's hand glowed much brighter now.

"So your hand says this way, right?"

Cale looked at his hand. It *seemed* to be saying this way. "Uh, well, it's not a real exact science you know, but yeah."

Ahead of the *Phoenix*, the cavern split into two smaller tunnels.

"Great. Well, could you maybe ask the hand if it's a left or a right up ahead?"

Cale looked at his hand. No clues there. "I'd say left." He paused. "No, maybe right."

"Cale . . ."

"Yeah, definitely right."

She snapped the ship to the right, putting an extra whip into it.

Touchy, touchy.

It wasn't his fault. Not like he *asked* for the job or anything.

Geez, Dad, you could have made different fingers blink or something.

After negotiating a short corridor, the *Phoenix* was in another cave, lined with gigantic and fantasic ice crystals. It was beautiful, but otherwise empty.

Ahead was an opening. Their ship went through, exiting back into space.

Cale felt a stab of disappointment. Nothing.

They came to a wall of particularly reflective ice crystals. Cale could see their ship's reflection. And off to the side—

"Hold it! Look there!"

"I don't see anything."

"The reflections! Akima, turn us around."

Akima banked the ship upward, and Cale saw it more clearly. A bronze blob lay behind a forest of refracting crystals.

"There! Head toward that!"

He felt a grudging admiration for his father as they worked their way toward the blob.

Smart, hiding it in a forest of mirrors.

Akima gasped. "Look! Have you ever seen anything like that?"

"Just once," Cale said. "A long time ago and far away."

They had found *Titan.*

– 24 –

The third problem she had been dreading began as Susquehana approached her chambers.

Assassins, and better this time: They were waiting at the junction just before the final connection to her chambers. Of course, she routinely scanned all the corridors within three junctions of her quarters so that she would not be taken by surprise, and thus she found them.

She scanned the mechanical camera viewers between herself and the junction to see if there were any other drones involved and received a shock.

One of the cameras was watching *her*.

Ah, they are better than the last attackers.

To infiltrate the Queen's surveillance system was a dangerous tactic, but one offering great potential. They would know her every move.

No matter. She had greater powers. Knowing her moves was not knowing her thoughts.

The Queen called up a visual manipulator codex and sent messages to every camera, up to and including her quarters.

Now *she* controlled everything the *conspirators* could see.

Of course, if they had managed to infiltrate her system, they might be aware that she had accessed the cameras at their junction, but that was unlikely. They could probably ill afford the concentration it took to manage one viewer. The power of the Orb made such things easy for her.

Still, best to leave nothing for chance to collect.

The Queen masked herself from view and took an alternate route. This was not what the conspirators would see. They would see her continuing to head their way.

As she walked, cloaked with focus-burners fully charged, she wondered who was behind the attack. Coming so close on the heels of the previous one, it was mildly surprising. The style that she had exhibited in disposing of that mess should have kept any smart contenders well back.

But this more complex attack seemed fully-formed. Almost as if it had already been in place when the last one happened. . . .

The lightning-fast brain that served the Queen came to a startling conclusion. *What if the last attack had been only a diversion? Logic would dictate both attempts were planned by the same drone.*

The Queen stopped mid-stride, stunned at the prospect.

Probing attacks? Meant to show my strengths and weaknesses?

It was a dark thought. Who among her drones had such resources and contacts? But it made sense. The last attack had been ended very swiftly, and the ostensible leader had been a relatively low-level drone.

This called for new tactics in her upcoming battle. If

this attack were meant to fail, there would be no need for the leader to be nearby because he would not believe the Orb would be available to consume.

But he *would* need to know what happened.

Carefully, she sent her awareness to the camera viewers that surrounded the conspirators. There were no obvious taps or split data streams.

This left two likely options: one, the drone was here.

She scanned the group below. There were two maintenance drones, three attack drones, and a *droheh*, no doubt leading the group.

The *droheh* was unknown to her. She did a quick check and found that his name was Sihalla, and he worked in one of the main data processing nodes. His background showed no brilliant thought, no proclivity toward deception.

No. The leader was not here. She was sure.

That left option number two: The leader of the group had an independent method of watching the events about to transpire. Precisely, and with great concentration, Susquehana used the cameras to scan every *rai* of the room. Nothing. All was accounted for.

Perhaps the viewers can't see it.

She tapped into the *droheh's* sightline and watched. He was split between watching her false image on the tap of her surveillance system and looking around the junction. Nothing exciting there. The drone gave nothing away.

Hmm. . . .

Perhaps one of the other drones? If this mastermind was so good, maybe he had *planned* for her to watch through the drone's eyes.

Time to be very careful indeed.

She tapped into all the remaining drones at once. The

data rolled over her in a wave and she immediately saw an irregularity.

One of the maintenance drones was *already* tapped!

It was a very minor fluctuation to be sure, and she wouldn't have noticed it had she not accessed the group as a whole and seen the variance.

She couldn't have been more surprised than if a bio-bod had suddenly jumped out of a wall and tried to eat her.

Someone else had figured out how to tap the sight lines of drones.

She attempted to trace the tap, but immediately it shut down.

Perhaps there is another way.

She reached the intersection with her image still a few corridors away and decloaked.

Immediately there were shots fired at her, high-speed, multiple passes.

But she was faster.

Zzzzzt. Zzzzt. Zzzzzzzt!

Her burners toasted the attack drones and disabled the maintenance drone who had been tapped.

He, however, must have been briefed on a situation like this. The drone rolled sideways and triggered a plasma torch, incinerating his brain.

Farg!

She needed survivors.

Carefully, she picked her way past the bodies and made her way to her chambers. Clearly, it was time to plan an offensive. In this situation, mere reaction seemed entirely too risky.

Once in her chambers, the portals sealed, the Queen considered the three problems she needed to solve. As usual, she ranked them by degree of danger to the race, and then herself.

There were two dangers to the race that needed immediate solutions. The first was related to the data carried by the drone she'd accidentally killed in the meeting chamber. The shielding situation for the white dwarf was deteriorating. The problem had grown so critical that there were now entire sections of *Alahenena* that were no longer habitable.

Worse, the ability of the ship to harness the power was fading. According to the report, the ship's capacity was down by 48 percent. This meant that the main weapons, the world-killers, were off-line, and that the propulsion system itself was at risk.

Not acceptable.

CONCUR

More power was required, *immediately.* Susquehana considered her options. There were really no choices. For the first time since Drej had arrived in this universe, they would have to generate power on their own to supplement the white dwarf.

She commed Qutarch, the power systems *droheh.*

"My Queen?"

"I have received your report concerning our power reserves. We must take extreme measures to serve the race. Bring on-line our backup antimatter generation systems and prepare other alternatives."

Qutarch's posture indicated shock. "We will need fuel—" he began.

"Do not bother me with such trifles. See that it is done."

"*Inastallah eair vey,*" he replied, in the formal manner. *I exist to serve.*

Yes, you certainly do.

Now, at least, they would have power. Projections indicated the backup systems were capable of bringing the ship up to near full capacity. She would have the world-killers when she found the *Titan*.

That was the second major problem. More than ever they needed the technology she suspected the ship held.

The drones who had analyzed the map had failed. Reviewing their data, Susquehana had discovered their fatal flaw: They had not taken into account the fact that the map was biokeyed—it would grow. Their shame had ended quickly—and fatally—when she realized their errors.

The *Titan* was no doubt in the Andali Nebula—*somewhere*. But it would take centuries to search the entire thing. She needed the ship *now*.

She decided to contact her agent.

First, preparation. The Queen commed Fantiquar. "Make ready a dozen cloaking scouts," she said.

"At once."

"Launch them on my signal toward the coordinates I set."

"Yes, my Queen."

She toggled the translation device on her commo and placed the call.

The biological's face, when it appeared on the commo screen was uglier than usual.

"Didn't I say not to call me here?"

"I am less concerned with your whims than I am with results."

The biobod got angry, as she had hoped it would. It shouted at her far longer than it should have. The time allowed her to triangulate the vector of his signal.

The place the humans call New Bangkok.

Another part of her intellect signaled Fantiquar to launch the spydrones.

She would not wait for this impertinent biobod to deliver the *Titan* to her. No. She would track him and take it. She commed Fantiquar again and told him to arrange for a jump near New Bangkok. She would be ready when the *Titan* was found.

Now it was time to consider the last of her three dark shadows.

The plotter.

She had been considering the problem as she dealt with the others. The Orb was technology of Artifact nature, and there were no others. It alone gave her the power to access the visual array of any of her subjects.

Still, logic was the overriding factor. If it were only possible that her drones could be read by the Orb, and they were being read without the Orb, there must be a second device of similar nature.

Since Artifact technology could only be created by the *Lanoor*, if there was a second device, it would have been created by one of the limited number of drones with access.

She immediately opened sight lines on all of them.

A myriad of images formed before her. One drone was eating, another was walking down a corridor, and another was sleeping. A fourth drone was walking slowly, his eyes downcast. He shuffled over to a wall and reached up. Without looking, he made an adjustment of some kind, and the edge of a boxlike shape crossed the corner of his vision.

Aha.

Susquehana seized control of a nearby camera.

It was Qutarch!

He was adjusting controls on the box before him. She had to acknowledge that he was good at nonshowing. His vision studied an image of power shields, but from the inanimate viewing point nearby, she could see him connecting leads to the box.

Abruptly Susquehana felt odd. It was as if her brain were seeing two of everything. . . .

He's seeing through my eyes!

Outrageous. Utterly outrageous.

FEEDBACK LOOP INITIATED

Pain began to shoot through the Queen's head.

He's using the device to interfere with the Orb!

Susquehana triggered her all-walls pass, shut her eyes, and began running. The pain got worse.

She shot through wall after wall, heading toward Qutarch's quarters. She kept her eyes shut as she ran, using her internal map of the ship to remain oriented.

His voice came into her head.

It is time for the Drej *to be led by one who will solve problems, not lead us on chases.*

You do not understand that of which you speak, she replied.

She had to distract him. *Watch.* Then she played the original scout's data on Sam Tucker; Qutarch was an engineer, he would figure it out.

I—I see your intentions are dutiful, yet I will prove stronger.

She pushed, trying to return the feedback loop to him.

Such a tactic is worthy, but doomed to fail. There is no direct connection to me, only you can be hurt.

She was nearly there, she could feel it.

Time to open her eyes.

She kept them down until she crossed into his chamber, and then looked up.

Qutarch looked at her, and it was like staring into infinity—she saw him looking at her, from his viewpoint and her own, on and on and on—

Until she fired the tri-split focus-burner she had grabbed before leaving her chambers.

ZZzzzzzppp!

His head exploded. She fired on the box.

It, too, made a satisfying display as it was destroyed.

Immediately the pain stopped. She stood there, triumph beginning to flow through her. Another threat to her—and thus to the race—defeated.

While she was still enjoying the glow of victory, Fantiquar contacted her.

"My Queen, I offer bright news."

"Bright news is welcome. Continue."

"We have found the *Titan*."

25

Cale watched the *Titan* grow larger and larger as the *Phoenix* moved in to dock. There was but a gentle tap as the two ships met.

Nice.

He was so excited that he wanted to jump up and down, but that would be childish. As soon as the two ships docked though, he tapped buttons on one of the consoles and checked the status of the *Titan*'s interior. Looked like the air was still good, but it was going to be stale. And *cold*.

He watched Akima go through shutdown procedures. Did she have to take so long?

At last she was done, and they headed for the airlock.

Within a few moments they were inside the *Titan*.

There was a feeling of vastness. They were in a long corridor that stretched into the darkness. A series of small lights indicated a route to a central platform. They walked through several storage areas as they followed the lights. He'd been right. It *was* cold. A plume of his breath wafted out in front of him, and he kept shivering.

"What exactly are we looking for?" asked Akima, her breath puffing out as well.

"This ship's going to help us save mankind."

"What *exactly* are we looking for?"

Cale grinned. "I don't have a *clue.*"

He stopped to take a look at one of the storage areas. There was an odd apparatus on a huge table. Rack after rack of containers and vials surrounded the table. Curious, Cale picked one up.

"DNA coding—Mammal, Tursiops Truncatus. The Bottle-nosed Dolphin."

He was silent for a second.

"Akima—these are—will be—animals."

She read some of the other containers. "Leopard, Elephant, Butterfly . . . looks like a regular Noah's ark here."

"Who?"

"Never mind, it's from an old legend about a transport ship full of animals."

Cale looked over at the central platform. Their arrival had activated some lights over there as well. He could see a desk and—

Look at that!

He rushed toward the steps leading up to the platform.

"Cale?"

"Over here!"

He ran up the steps toward the desk. There it was. His toy. The last time he'd seen it was the day the Earth had been destroyed. He'd thought it lost, as well.

He must have gone back for it. His father. With everything else at risk. . . .

Surrounding the toy were other things that sparked memories: his father's leather jacket, family photos, and some hard-copy letters that still had *stamps* on them.

His father had gone back for it. He had kept that toy.

It didn't take away all the pain he'd felt over the years, wondering when—or if—his father was going to come back, but it sure felt good. He looked at the makeshift paddle wheel and it was as if a door opened in his memory.

It had been a long day, but Cale wasn't ready to go to bed yet. For once, his daddy had not argued when he'd begged to stay up and work on his ship.

It was going to be so *great*.

Cale struggled to hold the gyro-floater still as he dabbed it with quickset liquid. His father sat nearby and offered suggestions.

"Nice one, son. Going to be a great floater, it is."

He'd grinned at his father.

Tek had wanted him to go outside and play on the grass. How boring! Only his father had stood up for him.

"If the boy wants to spend his time making a ship, let him. Can't say as I blame him—I like making things, too."

My daddy is just like me.

Young Cale had worked on the ship until his fingers could barely hold on to the floater. His father had come over and put his hand on his head.

"I think we've got a tired boy, here."

"Gotta finish it," he said. He yawned. "I *need* to."

So close, he'd been so close.

His father had sat down next to him and put Cale on his lap. "I'll help, son, if you want."

Cale yawned again, his eyelids drooping.

" 'Kay."

The next morning he'd awakened and rushed to see the floater. It was finished! His daddy had added the top part, and it was ready to be tested. . . .

●   ●   ●

"Dad . . ." Cale whispered.

Akima appeared beside him.

He looked down at where the paddle wheel had rested. There was a pad in the shape of a human hand, with a cone near each finger. Cale took his father's ring off and sat it on the cone of his ring finger, and then placed his hand on the pad.

Immediately lights began switching on, floor by floor. They illuminated the vast interior of the vessel.

Holy shit!

Cale heard fans kick in, and the air began to warm. He walked over to the railing at the edge of the platform and looked down at the lights blinking on. It was amazing.

Akima seemed just as amazed.

Abruptly there was a click behind them, and the two humans turned to see a figure take shape over the holo-proj on the control platform.

"Cale—" There was a pause.

It was his father!

"Dad?"

The boy moved towards the hologram, even though he realized it was only a recording. The holo didn't react to his new position as a live 'cast might.

"If this message has been activated, then I am probably dead." Again the holo paused, and a look of sorrow crossed his face. "I wish I could see you. I wish I could be there." The holo grinned. "You're probably taller than me by now."

Cale found his throat had gone dry.

"I don't know if you'll ever forgive me for leaving. I hope you understand that I had to. I had to keep you safe, son." He waited a beat. "Cale, this ship is mankind's salvation. It has the power to create a planet. To fill it with life, and to make a new home for Humans."

A planet!

Cale and Akima exchanged glances. They'd hit the jackpot.

The holo went on. "Your ring will activate the transformation sequence, but the *Titan*'s power cells were drained in the escape. It's up to you to restore power. After that, the procedure is relatively simple—

Abruptly a laser bolt flashed through the center of the holo, terminating at the projector. Cale's father vanished.

"He always did talk too much."

Cale spun. *Korso!*

— 26 —

C ale froze.

    Akima reacted faster. She pulled her weapon, but an expertly aimed blast sent it flying.

That would be Preed. Cale jerked his gaze to the side. Yes. There the ugly bastard was.

The Akrennian shook his head. "Sorry, I think not, Akima."

Cale finally thawed.

"Korso! Don't do this! This ship is all we have left! Doesn't that mean *anything* to you?"

Korso smiled, hard-edged. "Yeah, it means something. But I'm sorry, kid, somebody blowing up your home planet changes a man. You can't beat the Drej— no one can—they're pure energy. Let it go. You and Akima can walk away, but you've lost this one."

Cale shook his head. *What can we do? How can we stop him?*

He wasn't going down without a fight, but he wasn't inviting suicide, either.

"Actually," Preed said, "you've *all* lost. Please relieve

yourself of your firearm, if you will, hmm, Captain?"

Cale saw that the alien had put his gun to the back of Korso's head.

The older man was just as shocked.

"You backstabbing Akrennian bastard."

Preed smiled, his pointy teeth gleaming. "Well, I learned from the best, didn't I?"

Preed took Korso's weapon and tossed it over the edge of the control platform. Cale thought he heard the tinkle of glass breaking, far below, and wondered what species Preed had just doomed.

Of course, we're all pretty much doomed if we don't do something. He glared at the little alien.

"You sold me out."

"Well, yes, I did. But it wasn't just the money the Drej were offering, it was the health plan that came with it—" he paused. "They'll let me *live*, that's a big inducement. Of course, that's provided I kill all of you."

He cupped his hand around his ear theatrically. "Listen. Why, I think I hear them coming now."

He gave them that wolfish grin again. "Let's see—I don't know the proper etiquette for this sort of thing, so I'll just have to improvise as to who to blast first. I'll save you for last, Captain. Out of respect for our long association and all."

He pointed his gun at Cale, "Boy . . . ?" then at Akima. "Girl . . . ?"

He moved the gun back and forth. "Boy . . . girl . . . boy . . . so many choices. . . ."

Korso leaped over the railing of the control area.

"Stop!" Preed yelled. He leaned forward to track Korso, aimed—

Akima dived, slammed into Preed, spoiling his aim as he fired.

"Urk—!" The gun clattered onto the deck.

Akima kneed him in the stomach and doubled him over—go Akima—!

—but Preed smacked her head with one flailing elbow on his way down—

"Uhh—!" Akima fell—

Cale leaped at the Akrennian. He landed a hammer blow on Preed's shoulder, knocking him further off balance, then punched him in the side. Preed grunted.

Shoot *my* girl, will you—?

And then Cale saw a red flash and found himself on his back, stunned.

Preed had nailed him somehow—

Cale threw a weak punch, which the alien batted down effortlessly.

Preed glared down at him and growled. "Where is my damned—ah, there it is!" The Akrennian moved off Cale to recover his blaster.

Cale rolled up and scooted behind a bank of controls as Preed scooped his gun up and fired. He heard—and felt—the blast hit the panels. Heat singed his hair.

But there was no place to go from here, not without exposing himself to Preed's fire.

Bad. This was bad—

"Ahhh! Hide and seek? Or shall we call it—Search and destroy, hmm?"

Cale peeped out from his hiding place.

Preed cut loose again as Cale jerked back behind cover. The smell of burned plastic rolled over Cale in a cloud of fried control panel.

Things *really* didn't look good here—

Then he saw Korso clamber up over the railing behind Preed.

For the moment, at least, they had a common enemy.

So he stood up and shouted, "Hey, Preed, you ugly dickweed!" He ducked.

The Akrennian fired again. More scorched panels.
Wasn't doing the ship any good, Cale was sure, but better it than him—

"Ah!"

Cale popped up to see what had happened.

Korso stood there, his arm around the alien's throat.
The Akrennian's head was bent at a funny angle.

Korso had snapped Preed's neck. Preed was dead—
or would be soon enough.

Korso dropped the body as Cale dove for Preed's gun.

He grabbed the gun and pointed it at the older man.
Then he noticed that Korso held something in his hand.
It was his father's ring!

He needed that to start the activation sequence.

"Give me the ring, Korso."

Korso shook his head. "You're not going to shoot me,
kid. You haven't got it in you."

"Watch me."

But bad as he was, Cale didn't want to just shoot him
down. Maybe he could wound him. . . .

Korso came at him.

"Stop! I will shoot!"

Korso didn't slow.

Cale dropped his aim and fired a blast at the deck.
Maybe that would stop him—

It didn't. A second later, Korso was all over him. Cale
kicked and punched, the two of them grappled, wres-
tling, and Cale knew he was no match for the bigger
man.

No! It can't be like this!

Desperate, Cale twisted his hips, snapped his fist up,
and whacked Korso's head. The hit startled Korso. He
dropped the ring. There was a *ting* as it hit the floor.
Korso lost his balance and started to fall, but as he did,

he latched on to Cale, toppling them both over the edge of the control area.

Shiiit—!

They fell onto a catwalk, which had obviously not been designed to break the falls of a pair of fighting humans.

The catwalk collapsed—

Cale managed to grab on to the failing walkway.

Korso wasn't so lucky. The bigger man started to slide backward. The lower deck was a long way down, and Cale knew Korso wouldn't survive the fall.

For a heartbeat he didn't reach out. . . .

And then he did. He caught Korso's forearm as the captain dangled on the edge of the catwalk. Whatever else he was, Korso was a Human, like him. He couldn't allow him to fall. Not after New Bangkok.

"Hang on!"

Korso looked up at Cale, surprise in his eyes.

"You can let go, kid. I wouldn't blame you."

Cale tightened his grip, even as the older man began to slip.

He bit out the words: "No. I'm. Not. Going. To. Let. Go. . . ."

He tried. He really tried. But the weight was too much for his already tired body, and Korso slid loose and plummeted downward, falling through a tangle of loose catwalk cables before vanishing from view below the curvature of the inner sphere.

"Korso!"

But he was gone.

— 27 —

Cale lay on the catwalk, his heartbeat pounding in his ears.

Korso was gone. At least he had taken out Preed before he went.

He heard a familiar voice. "Anything broken, Human?"

Stith!

Cale inched his way up the catwalk until he was back near the stairs to the control area. He saw the Mantrin standing there with Akima. Apparently Korso and Preed were the only ones who had made a deal with the *Drej*— Stith wasn't pointing her gun at Akima, and they seemed to be on relatively friendly terms—as friendly as Stith got, anyway.

Good thing, too. He wouldn't have wanted to shoot it out with Stith. "Where is Gune?"

"On the *Valkyrie*, where he belongs," Stith said.

Akima asked, "You okay?"

Cale nodded. "Yeah."

"Korso?"

"Down there, somewhere." He pointed. "I didn't see him hit. We'll have to go find his body."

He saw the ring on the floor. He bent to pick it up— and fell over as the ship suddenly jolted to the side.

It didn't take a weatherman to know which way that wind blew. *The* Drej—*they're here!*

Cale looked at Akima. She looked as worried as he felt.

Susquehana watched the projection of the *Titan* from her tactical command chamber.

At last! I have found it, and I see it with my own eyes.

The way to reshape the destiny of the Drej in this galaxy was hers. All she had to do now was go and fetch it.

Preliminary scans indicated the ship was underpowered, its resources drained. But she would take no chances.

CONCUR

She spoke to the lead combat *droheh*, Tigaj. "Disarm the *Titan* and remove any means of escape."

"Yes, my Queen."

Tigaj activated comms and launched a phalanx of *slijah*. Their small weapons would disable but not destroy the huge vessel.

It had taken time and energy, but Susquehana had prevailed. Soon she would possess the means to make her legacy the greatest of any Drej Queen in this universe.

Her skin glowed with confidence. Her time had come.

Akima looked at the readouts of the sensors and started to head for the stairs.

Time to get outta here.

The Drej mothership had arrived and they were in

some deep shit. On a mostly unpowered vessel like this, they were waterbirds stuck on a frozen pond.

"Let's not panic," Cale said.

"Oh, really? We've got the Drej about to kick our asses, and we can't run and maybe we can't fight. Panic wouldn't be out of line here. We need to get to the *Valkyrie*. No way I'm gonna let myself be captured a second time to be ejected into space. Or worse. We have to get *gone!*"

"No. The safest place to be is right here."

Akima indicated the sensors. "You're crazy! Right *here* is about to be blown to pieces!"

Was he crazy? Did he have some kind of nonsurvival genetic disorder?

"Maybe," he said.

Maybe? *He's warped. Maybe I should knock him out and carry him.*

"Come *on,* Cale!"

"Wait! We can make this work! What did Korso say about the Drej?"

Akima stared at him. "We don't have time for word games!"

"What did he say?"

"That you can't beat them."

"Right. Because they're *pure energy.* And what does the *Titan* need right now?"

"A three-week head start wouldn't hurt. But we don't have the power."

Cale nodded. "Exactly. But if I can reroute the system to use Drej energy, it could start the reactor." He began to tap figures into the computer console. "And it might help us in other ways."

Akima stared. "You can't just *swipe* Drej energy!" She stared at him. "Can you?"

"I learned about manipulating it while I was on the

mothership. It's not as complex as it seems."

"Neither is getting hit by a blaster cannon! This is not the time for theoretical physics, Cale."

But he had already turned away and was playing with the controls. "The energy relays are linked to some circuit breakers, so this might do it. . . ."

"You *are* crazy. You really think this will work?"

He tapped a button, and the computer display lit up, followed by aural confirmation.

"<<Circuit breaker one. Engaged.>>"

"I hope so," he said.

The computer's voice continued. "<<circuit breaker two, Engaged.>>"

He might be able to pull this off—and when you got right down to it, what choice did they have? They might not even be able to get *to the* Valkyrie, *much less outrun the Drej.*

"<<circuit breaker three>>" There was a pause, "<<circuit breaker three, malfunction. Not engaged.>>"

"Dammit!" Cale frowned. He called up a view of a huge circuit breaker and stared at it. "Wait, wait, I can fix this!" He turned to Stith. "I gotta go outside. Can you cover me?"

"Ship has short-range capacitor-powered meteor blasters might can use," Stith said. "But popguns, like throwing stones." She grinned. "Of course, Stith *good* at throwing stones."

"Then throw them," Cale said. "I'm gone."

Akima stared at him, wanting more than ever before to be up *flying*.

Cale ran to an elevator. "Trust me on this, Akima! I just need a little time!" he said, punching the call button.

"How *much* time?" Akima yelled.

"A few hours."

Stith broke in. "Got a few *minutes*—*if* some deity owes you big favor—*and* if you are most lucky, too."

There was a chime, and the elevator door zipped open. Cale jumped in, and the doors quickly closed behind him.

Akima stared at the elevator. He seemed so *sure*.

Stith was already moving toward the gun controls, and Akima felt helpless. She hoped Cale knew what he was doing. Well. At least their ends would be cleaner than running out of air and slowly choking to death in a vacuum. Not much consolation, but you worked with what you had. . . .

-28-

Akima and Stith ran checks on the gunnery consoles. The *Titan* was well armed, but the lack of power limited them to just a few short-range weapons.

Akima checked the sensor readout. So far, the Drej vessel had launched only stingers.

So far. We just might be able to get Cale his time....

Stith hummed a martial tune as she ran checks on her gunnery console. The Mantrin seemed excited.

The first wave of stingers was on its way.

Akima felt a squeezing sensation and her vision seemed to narrow to the width of a pop straw. At the end of the tunnel she could see the stingers forming up for an attack run.

Relax, relax, be calm.

That was hard. She was used to a *moving* space battle. Stuck here on the *Titan* she felt like she was nothing but a big, fat target. Which, of course, they were.

Oh, gods, do I want to be flying.

She cleared her throat. "Here they come!"

Stith opened her beak in a move that looked like an

eagle about to drop on a fish. "Many will regret the day they met Stith."

The stingers came.

The battle was underway.

Once the elevator stopped, Cale jumped out and began to suit up. Tools, tools, he needed tools!

Over near the suit locker on the left there was a large box of zero-gee tools. He grabbed it and headed for the airlock.

It seemed to take forever as he waited for the outer airlock door to open. According to the schematic, the circuit breaker was near a large power coupling. The problem with schematics was that they only showed how things worked, not where they *were*. Cale began looking for something that would require a large power coupling.

Aha!

Over there, about a hundred yards distant was a large energy cannon. That seemed like a good candidate.

Akima's voice cut into his thoughts.

"Cale, let's move it!"

A series of explosions ripped into the deck nearby. Overhead, two Drej stingers seemed to be taking a personal interest in him.

Crap!

Doing his best to keep from lifting both boots off the ship and floating into space, Cale began to move at a speedy shuffle toward the cannon.

The Drej lined themselves up for an attack run.

Don't attack me *you idiots! You want a good* target, *aim for something else!*

The Drej apparently *didn't* want a good tactical target.

They swooped in. Ah, crap, things definitely did *not* look good for the home team here. . . .

One of the ships exploded, spiraling into the other

one, which also went up into a satisfying explosion.

"Guuuhhaarr!"

Thanks, Stith, I owe you.

But he wasn't out of danger yet.

Another stinger nosedived into the *Titan*. It was headed straight for him!

Desperately, Cale started backing up, trying to find a place he could hide.

The ship came on. Bits of the *Titan*'s ablative outer-hull plates sheared off and sprayed out from the ship.

Stith raked the attacker. The stinger wobbled. Slowed . . . but wouldn't be able to stop in time. . . .

Cale threw himself backward as the stinger smacked down right in front of him, tipping. The ship's nose dropped slightly as it stopped—and hooked him on his backpack of tools, pinning him to the ground like some kind of human butterfly.

He twisted and turned, trying to pull free, but it was not happening.

Akima called to check on him. "Cale? Cale? Are you okay?"

"Me? Oh, I'm just fine. I'm kind of . . . stuck, is all."

"Stith, who's outside with Cale?"

Outside? With me?

Uh-oh.

Cale started looking around, and wished he'd brought a gun.

Another *Titan* spacesuit clanked into view. The suit was larger than Cale's, and only one person could have filled it.

"Hi, kid."

Akima heard, too. "Korso?" she said.

Cale looked up at the older man. "Well, you'll never have an easier shot than this."

The bigger man grinned. Cale was amazed that he

could see it from this angle; it was funny how clear and sharp everything had become. Fascinated, he watched as Korso pointed his weapon toward him. He noticed every detail as Korso's trigger finger slowly squeezed—

And fired—

But the blaster bolt flew *past* him—and into the Drej pilot who was climbing from the wreckage!

Another Drej emerged a second later—and got the same treatment.

Then the older man turned his blaster on the wreckage pinning Cale to the ground. A few carefully placed shots and the boy was free.

"What the hell, kid. Maybe we can beat them after all."

Cale was stunned. "Uhh—?"

Korso began plinking at other stingers. The handgun didn't do much damage, but at least he was shooting at them and not Cale.

"Go on, get to work, kid. I'll cover you."

What the hell. Cale went.

Stith fired thousands of low-powered shots at the attacking stingers. Akima joined her at the console, and discovered that the intense focus required for gunnery was a bit like flying. She could see why Stith enjoyed this.

The Mantrin was in ecstasy. She hummed battle hymns as she targeted the attacking ships, punctuating odd notes with victory cries. Stith was in her element.

The backup holoprojector showed the exposed surface of the *Titan*. Only a portion of the ship was exposed to space, with the rest encased in a thick, protective sheet of ice that had built up over the years. This was a plus because it meant they had less area to cover. On the other hand, it also gave the Drej fewer targets to attack.

Two tiny figures were visible on the exposed side of

the projection: one was Cale, working at the base of one of the laser cannons, and the other was Korso. Akima had hardly believed it when she'd heard his voice on the commo. *Alive!* And he'd decided to help them! What had brought on his change of heart? It didn't matter. He'd saved Cale.

Three triads of stingers started an attack run toward Akima's last gun. She'd had ten to start with and had used auto-targeting on most of them, jumping around from gun to gun to add that little bit of unpredictability to her fire patterns. Underneath the holo was her targeting screen, and it showed a first-person view of the incoming fighters. She toggled the joystick that rotated the cannon's point of aim and took out the lead ship in the second triad. One of the two following managed to avoid the debris of the lead ship, but the other was caught and exploded.

Yeah!

Unfortunately, the first triad had reached targeting position and let loose at her cannon. Her shield matrix flexed and held, and she managed to get the lead ship in the third group before the shield gave way. Then her display went blank.

Damn.

She turned toward Stith just as the Mantrin said, "Fantastic, I only two guns left!" Far from concerned, the alien seemed *excited* at the prospect of facing the Drej with fewer weapons. Like she needed the handicap.

"Take starboard gun," Stith said.

Akima assigned it to her console.

Cale stood at the base of the laser cannon, the access panel for the manual override finally open. He'd never had so much trouble with a screwdriver before, and once he'd gotten two of the screws free, he took a crowbar to the panel and peeled it back. He figured he'd fix it later, if there *was* a later.

There was the override activation switch. He reached in and grabbed the small handle, turning it 90 degrees. If this worked, the breaker would close, the shield emitters would effectively become collectors, and with the parameter adjustments he'd made in the computer, they *should* be able to collect the particular frequency of the Drej weapons' energy.

He hoped.

He looked at the circuit breaker. No change yet. And then he saw the flashing red light and knew the override had failed.

Shit!

He *always* got the backup that wouldn't work!

Screw it. He'd do it manually.

He reached up and grabbed the activation arm for the breaker. He pulled, trying to snap it shut.

Of course, it didn't budge. Of course.

The stinger exploded and Akima grinned.

"Gotcha!"

Here came three more. She fired at them and abruptly heard nothing but the click of her triggers. The pilot slammed her fists on the weapons console. Out! Dammit, she was *out*. Stingers flew past her dead cannon, not even bothering to blow it up.

Cale looked at the breaker. He used the crowbar as a lever, trying to get the actuator arm to move. All of his strength went into it, legs, back, arms.

The wall of the box bent.

"Ah, *dammit!*"

Okay, okay, he'd try the other side—

• • •

The Queen studied her tactical holo.

Her *slijah* weren't being nearly as effective as she had hoped. Neither the propulsion nor the primary weapons had been knocked out yet. The biobods were proving particularly resourceful.

They have nowhere to run. Even darkness attacks the light when cornered.

Apparently her agent had failed. It was not much of a surprise. They were so unreliable, the biologicals. Perhaps she could make their situation hopeless and cause them to "give up." The Queen flashed amusement at the thought. The concept of "giving up" was so very alien. When your enemies were extinguished, then you had no enemies. Taking prisoners was a *biological* fallacy.

The majority of the *Titan* was covered in a huge, ice sheet that served as a shield. Should it be removed, there would be no way the humans could protect the entire craft, limited as their numbers were.

"Stand by the main burners; destroy the ice shield with minimal penetration."

She would show them how futile it was to resist the Drej.

Stith was approaching the end of her weapon's energy.

"Rrrrrraaaahhhhhh! Come to Stith, come and die!" she shouted at the stingers. "Rrraahh!"

A look of fierce concentration came over the Mantrin's face. Stith toggled a switch and split the control for her dual energy cannon into two aiming points. Her hands took a joystick each.

Akima watched, amazed. She'd known the Mantrin was good, but this was unbelievable. Stingers attacked, and stingers died. The console showed fifty stingers in the attack wave, and their numbers dropped to zero just as the alien's triggers clicked empty.

"Excellent shooting, Stith. Excellent."

Another wave started in.

"A most glorious battle," said Stith. "Now we die." She seemed satisfied with herself. She beamed at Akima.

Akima nodded.

It certainly looked as if it was all over. She hoped she had time to tell Cale good-bye. . . .

—29—

Cale stared at the breaker. *Damn!* What would it *take* to get it closed?

"Cale, we've got a problem here." It was Korso, right behind him.

"Tell me about it. It won't move."

Korso took his shoulder and turned Cale around. The Drej attack ships were starting to return to the distant mothership. They were leaving? How was that a problem? That was good news, right?

Korso pointed at the distant airlock. "Come on, you have to go. You have to get to cover."

"Why? They aren't shooting!"

"Cale, they're pulling back."

"Hey, I'm not blind, I can see that."

"Why do you think they're *doing* that?"

He'd been concentrating on the problem at hand, and it didn't register. "I give up."

"To get out of the way so the mothership can fire the big guns."

"Oh."

"Yeah. You need to get more than just a suit between you and them."

"*I* do?" He looked at Korso. "What about you? *You* can't stay out here, either."

Korso shook his head. "I'll take care of it. You man the activator."

Cale didn't move. Korso reached over and grabbed him. "Go."

He was torn. Someone would eventually have to go back to activate the transformation sequence, but—

"Cale, where are you?" Akima.

Korso leaned closer, "Go. It's better this way."

The boy nodded and started for the airlock.

Halfway there, he commed Korso. "How's it coming?"

Korso grunted. "Nearly got it. . . ."

He was almost to the airlock, when he stumbled and fell. Nearly all of the stingers were gone, but a stray trio, the last ones still out there, made a final pass in his direction.

Oh, man.

Plasma bursts pocked the *Titan*'s hull, working their way toward him. He scrambled to get to his feet, but in the back of his mind he knew he wouldn't make it.

Cale looked up and watched the stingers. If he was going to go, he wanted to see it coming.

Instead, what he saw were the stingers exploding.

What the—?

It was the *Valkyrie*! A voice he hadn't heard in a while came over the commo, "Hello, Friends."

"Gune!"

The little alien went on. "Okay I blow up stinger ships, yes?"

The *Valkyrie* took off after the remaining stingers.

Cale entered the airlock and ran straight for the elevator, not bothering to take off his spacesuit.

Susquehana stared at the reports from her scouts. Apparently the Humans were attempting to alter the circuitry on the *Titan*.

Why?

Could she afford to wait and find out?

NO

The Orb was right. It was best to be safe. The *Alahenena* was operating nearly at full power. They could do without the technology. Another way for repairs could be found. A pity to lose it, but safety was paramount.

CONCUR

She toggled the comms. "Position to destroy."

— 30 —

Cale dashed across the deck toward the activation controls.

The ring! Come on, get the ring!

Cale yanked off the spacesuit gauntlet and tugged on the ring.

"Come on, come on, come on—!"

The Queen watched the tactical display console. The *slijah* had rejoined the ship and reformed into their world-destroyer formation.

She commed Tigaj. "Lock on the *Titan*."

"Yes, my Queen."

The *droheh* continued to give orders. "Adjust spatial divergence to one hundred *anarai*. Activate *inaji* reservoirs."

Now we finish it.

Cale watched a viewscreen that showed the breaker outside on the hull. It still wasn't closed.

Damn!

Abruptly Korso stepped into the picture and thrust his pry bar between the two sides of the breaker. There was a spark—

Now why didn't I think of that?

And Cale turned to activate the transformation sequence.

Akima watched a series of screens. On the main holoprojection, she saw the Drej ship readying its main guns. A halo of blue fire began to surround the mothership. The fire started to extend a tendril toward the *Titan*. On a smaller screen, the pilot saw Korso jam the metal pry bar between the breakers and she watched in horror as the first tendrils of the Drej energy weapon touched the hull of the *Titan*.

Korso disappeared in the blue fire, shaking his fist at the Drej, defiant until he disappeared.

Turned out he wasn't so bad in the end.

Cale slapped the ring down on the activation cone and smiled when he saw a small spark jump.

Good job, Korso.

He watched the readouts on the transformation process. If he'd timed it wrong, they were screwed. . . .

No. The transfer was working. There wasn't much yet, but it would come. Cale took a glance up at the holoprojection. The Drej energy was hitting the *Titan*. . . .

Now.

There was a spike in the reactor readings, and abruptly a large laser mounted across from the control area came to life. There was a radiant shock wave as the gun ignited.

Cale, Akima, and Stith were blown backward by the blast.

When he stood up again, he saw that there were three beams of laser light converging in the center of the *Titan*. He checked the readings on the transformation console. The energy cells were running well within variance—they were in no danger of overloading.

Good.

Then, from the convergence point of the three lasers, another beam of light began to descend toward the odd apparatus he and Akima had seen at the bottom of the ship.

The ring control unit suddenly spun clockwise and an orange glow began to come from the it.

Cale grinned. It was working.

A readout flashed: GENESIS CHAMBER ON-LINE.

The two humans and the Mantrin leaned over the railing and looked down at the chamber far below.

The large energy beam from the lasers swirled around the chamber. A cone-shaped device caught the energy and began to spin it in the opposite direction.

Cale watched as the beam, now a different color, arced up to the nexus where the other beams had converged and to the main laser. Fascinated, he watched as the laser fired a reddish beam that didn't look like anything he'd ever seen before. The beam traveled through an optically clear portal that had irised open on the opposite side of the ship. That was new, too. He looked at the holo and saw the beam heading straight for the Drej ship.

This is interesting—

Susquehana watched the red beam approach the *Alahenena* and for the first time since she'd become Queen, felt real fear.

What is that?

The beam was fast, and as she watched in horror, it

laid out hundreds of light tendrils on the surface of the *Alahenena*.

And she *hurt*.

"Something's wrong! Cease fire! Cease fire! CEASE FIRE!"

*CON—

The Orb did not complete the word.

Because the Orb was . . . *gone*—

No!

It was worse than she had thought. Tigaj *couldn't* cease fire. Susquehana watched him tapping controls and issuing orders, all to no avail.

She fired a focus-burner at him, ending his fruitless activity.

She watched as bolts of energy began to fly between the walls and floors. The carefully controlled matrix of the *Alahenena* broke down.

Drones began to stretch and elongate, much as they did during a Making. They began to grow smaller, too, as if they were being unmade.

The Queen nodded at this final irony. *We're* being used.

"It's *absorbing* ussssssssss. . . ."

Cale switched his attention between the holo and the readouts on the transformation controls.

Why bother? I have no idea what it's doing.

Good point. He stepped back and watched. It was an incredible show.

The energy exchange between the Drej ship and the *Titan* seemed to be reaching some kind of climax. Multicolored beams of light shot off in all directions and there was a kind of . . . red coating on a large section of the mothership.

Suddenly the Drej ship seemed to collapse in on itself,

and there was a major increase in the intensity of the beams flowing toward the *Titan*.

The Drej, the ship, they were just . . . gone.

There was a huge explosion of light from the *Titan*. Ice from the surrounding rings shot off in all directions. There was now a space in the center of the ice field.

Big enough for a planet.

A huge swirling mass of gas appeared at the center of the space. Beams of light from the *Titan* pushed into it, manipulating the mass, adjusting. As Cale watched, the shape began to take on a more solid form.

It's collecting mass.

The now-solid sphere continued to collect ice, gas, and particles of solid matter, from who-knew-where. It continued to grow, becoming a molten ball. Cale was reminded of all the science classes he'd ever taken that described the formation of a new planet. But speeded up by billions of times. Absolutely unbelievable.

A planet. Nice work, Dad.

The mass cooled and clouds began to form. Tiny lightning bolts flashed all over the sky of the quickly evolving world.

It couldn't be happening, not according to physics as Cale had learned it, but there it was, growing and changing and *becoming*.

The energy bursts continued, and when they finished, there, in front of the *Titan* lay the greatest achievement any engineer could have ever dreamed up:

A new planet.

—EPILOGUE—

C ale and Akima walked on the surface of the new planet. It had taken a week for the formation of the world to be completed, and Akima told Cale she knew a bit about his father's sense of humor.

Seven days. She said she'd explain it later.

So he and Akima were the first to set foot on the virgin world.

It was gorgeous. Soil had already sprouted grasses, although most of what they saw was cliffs and rocky areas. In time, there would be more growth. A lush-looking lake stretched out, far below their vantage point.

Akima smiled. "This is not possible, you know."

"I hear that."

Her voice took on a more serious tone. "What are you going to call it?"

Cale paused. Hmm.

"I think I'll call it—Bob."

"Bob?"

Cale grinned. "What's the matter? You don't like Bob?"

Akima shook her head. "You can't name a *planet* Bob!"

"Oh," said the boy, "so now you're the boss? *You're* the king of Bob?"

"Well, no, but—"

"What?"

"Can't you just call it *Earth*?"

Cale smiled and looked at her. She was smiling, too. He took her hand.

"Well," he said, "I'm going to call it Bob."

She glared. "I'm *never* calling it that."

But they grinned at each other. Cale couldn't imagine anything better than this. A new world, and a woman with whom to share it. They'd have it all to themselves, at least for a little while. *Thanks, Dad.*

She moved a little closer, and he leaned over—

And just as they were *finally* about to kiss, a ship blew past, and the sonic boom nearly shook them off the cliff.

It was, of course, the *Valkyrie.*

"I *hate* you, Gune!" Cale yelled. He saluted the ship with one finger.

On board, they knew, Stith and Gune would be heading out to spread the news about humanity's new home. And there wouldn't be any Drej bothering them, at least not for a while.

Cale smiled and held Akima's hand.

It was good to be home.

And this time, nothing interrupted the kiss, which lasted a long, long time.

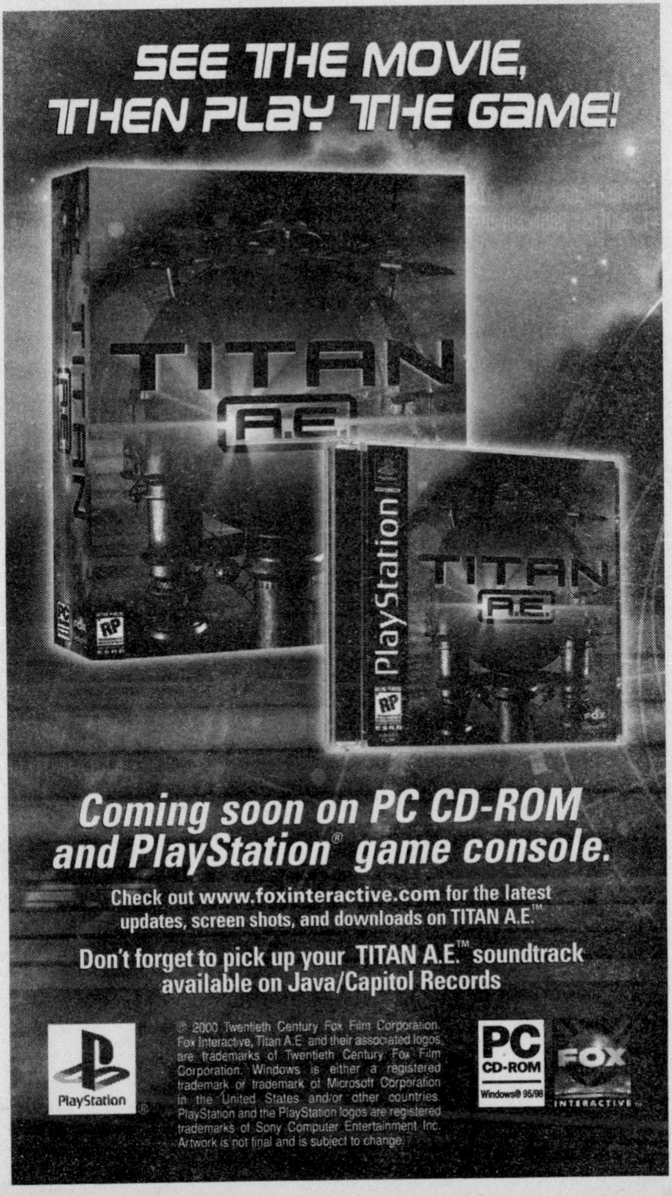
SEE THE MOVIE,
THEN PLAY THE GAME!
TITAN
A.E.
PlayStation
TITAN
A.E.
Coming soon on PC CD-ROM
and PlayStation® game console.
Check out www.foxinteractive.com for the latest
updates, screen shots, and downloads on TITAN A.E.™
Don't forget to pick up your TITAN A.E.™ soundtrack
available on Java/Capitol Records
PlayStation
© 2000 Twentieth Century Fox Film Corporation. Fox Interactive, Titan A.E. and their associated logos are trademarks of Twentieth Century Fox Film Corporation. Windows is either a registered trademark or trademark of Microsoft Corporation in the United States and/or other countries. PlayStation and the PlayStation logos are registered trademarks of Sony Computer Entertainment Inc. Artwork is not final and is subject to change.
PC
CD-ROM
Windows® 95/98
FOX
INTERACTIVE